LOUIS'
REVENGE

RICK JOYCE

ISBN 978-1-909121-67-6

www.acornindependentpress.com

ACKNOWLEDGEMENTS

I would like to thank the following people for their hard work and devotion, which helped to make this book a reality.

Sue and everyone at the Essex Horse and Pony Protection Society (EHPPS) for their commitment to rescuing and homing horses and ponies throughout the year, come rain or shine. Shelley and Lyn for their dedication to preparing the horses and ponies for their new homes. Renata for her fantastic illustrations, which bring the book to life. Lesley for her help with fine-tuning the story. Leila and Ali (my publishers) for their continued guidance. And above all, Louis-Springer and Bobby (the two on the cover) for being such wonderful and charismatic horses.

ABOUT RICK JOYCE

This book has been inspired by the sad reality that many people who mistreat horses and other animals manage to get away with it.

Louis' Revenge is based loosely on true life events, and much of the early chapters are a true account of what happened to Rick's horse, Louis-Springer (Lou). It amazes everyone who was part of Lou's rescue and rehabilitation that he is now so placid and friendly given the suffering he experienced in his early life. Rick spends time with Lou everyday and enjoys the affection that Lou offers in return.

Rick Joyce (who is actually John in this story) decided to write this book to highlight some of the devastating situations faced by real people in the animal welfare sector on a day-to-day basis. His daughter, Shelley, works as a horse trainer for private clients and also as a volunteer horse trainer for Essex Horse and Pony Protection Society. She first introduced Rick to Lou in November 2012 and by March 2013 he had fostered him. This process has given Rick both a love of horses and also a deep understanding of their dependency on human beings.

I dedicate this book to everyone
involved in animal welfare

LOUIS' REVENGE

RICK JOYCE

I

A SAD FAREWELL

Jack, a little Hackney horse was born into a family who couldn't afford to keep another one. Jack was a beautiful horse and so adorable with his long eyelashes and the white patches on his legs made it look like he had three white socks. He had a jet-black mane and tail, a little white mark just under his belly on the right-hand side, which stood out from the dark brown hair on his body.

He had a very distinctive white diamond shape patch between his eyes and two little stripes on the end of his nose, which made him look so cute.

Jack's mother, Hope, was also a beautiful bay coloured horse but the white patches on her legs made it look like she had four white socks. Jack had inherited so much of his mother's features including her long black mane and tail.

She was kept purely for riding and was very well looked after by her owners' twelve-year-old daughter, Atalia.

Atalia loved Jack and ever since he was born she spent as much time grooming him and caring for him as she could. She knew that they couldn't afford another horse and that he would have to be sold at some point; she did not want him to go, but it was out of her hands.

Jack in return enjoyed being brushed and cared for by Atalia; she was the first human that he ever met and he thought that they would all be as kind as her.

Hope and Jack had their own sizeable stable and paddock and she and Jack were often allowed into the neighbouring fields to be with other horses and to graze on the fresh grass that the larger field had to offer. Jack loved these visits to the large fields and although he stuck by Hope's side most of the time, he was allowed to venture off to play with some of the other younger horses. Hope enjoyed watching Jack grow and she found it quite amusing when one of the more mature horses would chase Jack off. Jack would run back to her as fast as his little legs could carry him. It was good for Jack to understand that there is a hierarchy amongst horses; one day it would be his turn to show his standing.

Jack wouldn't need his mother's milk for much longer and Hope knew that Jack would be taken from her soon. She had to give him the very best advice that she could to prepare him for his future.

'Now then Jack,' she started with tears welling up in her eyes, 'there comes a time in a young horse's life when he is likely to be taken to a new home. It happens as soon as he no longer relies on his mother's milk.' Hope found it very difficult to speak to Jack as he ate the fresh grass and barely listening to what his mother was saying.

'Look at me please, Jack,' said Hope softly. Jack looked up and saw a look on his mother's face that he had not seen before, and then he spotted a tear running down his mother's cheek. He had never seen that before. Hope was always happy, they both were.

'What's wrong?' said Jack as he looked at his mother. 'You look sad.'

Hope composed herself and continued. 'I'm trying to tell you Jack, that the time has nearly come for you to start your own life.'

Jack looked at his mother still not sure of what she was trying to say. 'What does that mean?' said Jack excitedly. 'Will I get my own stable now and get to play with the horses in the other fields?'

Jack was so innocent and never dreamt for one minute that he would ever be parted from his mother.

'No Jack, it means you will have someone else looking after you, but it also means that you will no longer be with me.'

The sudden realisation of what his mother had just said shook Jack to the core.

'But Mum, who will look after me when I'm not well?' As the tears continued to run from Hope's eyes, Jack knew that it wasn't going to be her. 'But Mum what have I done to be taken from you? I've been good, haven't I?'

Jack was crying now and his head hung low as Hope tried to explain things to him.

Jack soon understood that keeping a horse costs the owner a lot of money and that it was not his or his mother's fault. It was just the way it was: he would have to be sold. His owners would find some new people to look after him.

Hope spent her last couple of days with Jack telling him how to behave as a young horse, and that the more he listened to his master the better he would be treated.

Their owners put an advert in the local paper and horse magazines. Times were hard and horses were easy to come by, so it was no wonder that the asking price was not met. Several offers were made but eventually the owners knew they would have to accept half of what they had hoped for.

So the day came. Jack was just eight months old when he was sold and despite the pleasant couple that bought him and who said that they wanted to train him up for shows and dressage, their real intent was something quite different.

It was late morning and Jack was loaded into the small trailer just as his mother told him he would be. He behaved himself and went quietly. Hope was standing in her paddock looking on with her heart broken, with tears streaming down her cheeks. Despite wanting to let out the loudest cry she could, she just murmured, 'Goodbye little one, you made me a proud mum.' Jack was crying too as he was driven away, but he promised Hope that he would be strong for her and keep quiet. Jack also promised his mother that he would never forget her and that when he grew up he would come and visit her.

When Jack arrived at what would be his new home, his new masters seemed kind and caring as they led him out into a small muddy paddock with no shelter other than that of a wide oak tree.

Jack looked around and expected to see a nice warm stable with some hard-standing where he would be groomed by his master while eating fresh hay from a hay net. Jack assumed that he must have been put into a temporary paddock while they unloaded his rugs and other personal things like his grooming kit, feed and water bucket.

Jack walked around and it was clear that there had been a horse in the paddock before, which made him wonder where it was now.

It soon became obvious to Jack that this was it: his new home. 'Why don't I have a stable like my Mum's?' he asked himself. Although there was a large heap of straw on the ground under the oak tree for him to lie on, this was soon to become wet and uncomfortable.

As the day wore on, Jack wondered what he had done to deserve such a poor home and to be left so alone and frightened. It was now early afternoon and since he had been put into the paddock he had neither seen nor heard anything of his new owners. He walked around and occasionally heard the sound of cars passing by the country lane in front of the paddock. As soon as he heard the cars coming he would run to the back of the paddock, as he had never seen these metal monsters before.

As late afternoon turned into early evening and the sun started to go down, Jack became more and more apprehensive about the prospect of his first night in the paddock alone. He had never once spent a night on his own, especially without the surroundings of a nice warm stable.

As the light faded, Jack sought comfort from the protection that the oak tree offered. He eventually lay down on the bed of straw that offered some warmth from the cold ground and cried himself to sleep. That night was one of the worst that he had ever experienced. The odd cars that passed by and the distant howling of a dog woke him so many times that he barely slept that night.

The next morning Jack was given a small feed bucket containing chaff and a few carrots with some pony nuts, which was less appetising than anything he had ever had before.

Later that day he was given a hay net and introduced to Billy, the boy who was supposed to be looking after him. It seemed the couple that had collected Jack wouldn't be interested until he was much bigger and stronger.

Billy knew nothing about horses and although he seemed to like Jack at first, he was never kind to him.

The small hay net that he was given was soon gone and he had to forage for small tufts of grass that were in the bare paddock. The field beyond the back of the paddock looked so inviting to Jack with its fresh grass and space to run around.

Jack missed the company of his mother and he found himself once again crying and thinking of all the fun he had enjoyed before he came to this place. All Jack could do was wander around the paddock and think about his past.

A little black and white cat jumped up onto the fence at the front of the paddock, which caught Jack's eye. Jack slowly wandered over to the cat and was glad to have some company.

'My name's Jack,' he said in a sombre tone. 'What's yours?'

'I'm Scamp,' said the little cat who was also pleased to have some company.

The two new friends chatted about where they had come

from and Jack soon found out that Scamp was the same age as himself and had only been there for two weeks.

Scamp lived in the house and had his own comfortable bed; Jack felt quite jealous.

When it was time for Scamp to go in for dinner, Jack got quite upset at the thought of being alone again, 'Please come back and see me as soon as you can,' he said as Scamp jumped down and wandered off.

'Don't worry Jack I'll come back and see you whenever I can.'

The rest of the second day and night were exactly the same as the day before and Jack again cried himself to sleep, although he had started to accept that perhaps this was how it was going to be from now on.

Days turned into weeks and weeks turned into months for Jack and it was exactly the same each and every day. The only enjoyment that he had was the time he spent with Scamp. They would spend hours talking about their past and what Scamp had been up to.

Scamp was the sort that liked to exaggerate and he would tell Jack how he had scared off a dog that came into the garden and how he would chase all of the birds out of the surrounding fields, 'including the big black ones' he would say in order to sound tough.

Jack loved to listen to Scamp's tales and the more Jack enjoyed his stories the more far-fetched they became. It was the highlight of Jack's day when Scamp came around, although it did make Jack miss having the freedom that Scamp had.

The straw bed that Jack slept on was only changed when it was absolutely sodden wet and muddy. Although Jack was given a rug to wear during the cold winter nights, that soon became heavy with mud and water. The rug rubbed on his neck and wore away his hair causing his skin to become very sore.

Only occasionally, and when he could hardly walk, would his hooves be trimmed. Billy didn't get a qualified farrier to carry out the trimming and more than a few times Jack was left with uneven hooves and very sore feet. Jack felt so abandoned and often questioned why it was that he had been taken away from his mother to a life of misery.

Jack received no training or schooling during the eight months he had been at his new home and at the age of sixteen months when he had grown to a modest twelve hands he was put into a two wheeled trap by Billy that was far too big for him to pull. He tried to resist being strapped to the strange looking thing but was beaten by Billy with a short whip which stung him really badly and left marks and bruises wherever he was hit.

Jack looked at the contraption as he was being harnessed to it with absolute fear. It had two wheels with a seat mounted in the middle and long wooden poles that ran down the side of Jack's body which were harnessed to him by various collars and straps around his neck and back.

Billy's dad had grown up with horses and had raced them with traps for money. His plan was for his son to race Jack; only Billy had no idea how to race and Jack wasn't strong enough.

Because Jack was new to having a trap harnessed to him, Billy decided to take him into the field beyond the paddock where there was plenty of room.

Billy's dad had learnt horse and trap racing on his own and apart from providing them for Billy, he gave his son no tuition at all.

Billy would use the whip to excess and shout and scream

at Jack to go faster in the field. The reins and wooden arms of the contraption that he was harnessed to made him quite sore and every day he was in some sort of pain.

Jack was frightened to the core at the treatment that he was subjected to on a daily basis.

He wasn't cared for or even trained properly, he was just expected to know what to do. When he got it wrong he was hit all over his body with the whip that he had begun to fear, he was shouted at endlessly but the whip was one of the worst things that he had ever experienced and despite trying his hardest he couldn't please Billy for weeks but eventually he worked out what was expected of him.

He had remembered what his mum had told him: 'The more he listened to his master the better he would be treated,' she had said just before they were parted. Although he trusted his mother's words things were getting much worse even though he was being good.

As he became stronger and more responsive, although still very much underweight for his size, so the whip became more painful on his back.

In an attempt to make him go faster when he had mastered pulling the trap with Billy sitting on top of it, the whip was used more.

On one occasion Billy took Jack on the quiet country lanes where the trap racing would sometimes take place; Billy wanted Jack to get used to the hard surface before entering him into a race.

This was to be one of the worst experiences that Jack had ever had to endure.

As Billy drove Jack on up the road he started to pick up a good speed, the cracking of the end of the whip on Jack's back made him want to escape it and for Billy it was having the desired effect.

Billy had only ever taken Jack into the fields in the trap

where there was plenty of room to turn and visibility was good. It was very different on the country lanes with the high hedges and sharp turns in the road.

Billy was young and foolish and wanted to impress his dad by telling him that he was ready to start racing Jack and that he had been training him on the road.

As they approached a bend in the road, Billy kept his whip slashing at Jack's back instead of slowing him down.

'Faster Jack, faster,' he would shout. This was the start of a series of events that would haunt Jack for the rest of his life.

Billy suddenly realised that the bend in the road was far too sharp for them to negotiate at the speed Jack was pulling the trap and he pulled on the reins as hard as he could to slow Jack down.

'Whoa Jack, whoa boy,' Billy shouted in a panic stricken voice. It was too late, the momentum of the trap and sharpness of the corner was too much for them. The trap slid across the road and slammed into the mud bank while Jack struggled to maintain his footing and stay upright.

It was of no use, the wheel buckled under the impact and the trap bounced up in the air flipping Billy completely out of his seat.

The trap, now so much lighter started to turn in the air and the poles running down the side of Jack's body made it even harder for him to stay on his feet. It was too late, Jack was over and sliding along the floor with the trap coming down on top of him.

When Jack and the trap came to rest there was a strange silence that frightened Jack. He could feel the trap on top of him and as hard as he tried to move he couldn't.

Eventually he could see that Billy was unbuckling the straps and harnesses that were stopping him from moving.

'Come on Jack, up you get boy, please.' This was the first

time since Jack was introduced to Billy that he had ever heard his voice sound friendly.

Fortunately for Billy and for Jack neither was seriously hurt, although the slashing of the whip on Jack's back was damage enough.

This experience was the last thing that Jack was prepared to take and when he was back in his muddy paddock he started to think how he might escape.

As the trap was broken he was spared the daily routine of being harnessed up to it and the awful experience he had been through when it crashed on top of him. He really knew he had to end this misery.

His hooves were becoming longer and causing him to walk in a way that was not natural and when he could take no more, as he approached his second birthday, he knew he had to escape the torture. One side of the paddock had a solid wooden fence that faced onto a quiet country road that saw hardly any traffic, two sides of the paddock had high hedgerows and on the remaining side were a high barbed wire fence and an entrance gate. It would be very difficult to escape and he had no idea where he was.

One rainy day he decided that he would just charge into the barbed wire fence that was a barrier to him and freedom and push his way through. He walked up to the fence and sniffed it as if it was a living thing and having smelt no danger he was sure it was safe to charge down, but he didn't know what damage the barbed wire could do.

He went as far back to the other side of the little paddock as he could and started his run. As he ran through the fence, which buckled under his strength, the barbed wire stuck to him.

His legs and chest were ripped open like a paper bag, but such was the adrenaline racing through him that he just kept on running. The barbed wire and two posts were tangled up around his legs but he refused to stop. He was free.

Eventually the barbed wire and posts let go of their hold on Jack, but not before collecting tufts of his flesh and hair.

His short journey through the quiet field seemed like heaven until he reached a low wooden fence that he knew he would not be able to break through. Undeterred he circled a few times and came up with a plan.

As he approached as fast as his aching, bloody and worn out legs would take him, he leaped as high as he could and cleared the fence with ease but Jack was in more danger than he realised.

He found himself on a quiet road, which scared him enormously as he had seen vehicles or 'monsters' passing at speed on the road outside of his old paddock as he had described them to Scamp. He was also reminded of how the trap had folded on top of him when he had been on the road for the first time. But he was just happy to be rid of the squalor that his owners thought was good enough for him. He was starting to feel the pain now and was very tired so he walked apprehensively up the road, ears pricked up and eyes looking everywhere and wondered where his path would take him.

He passed by several fields where there were other big and mature horses with beautiful coloured rugs that came right up to the top of their necks to keep them nice and warm. The horses wandered over to the edge of the field to take a closer look at this scruffy little horse and wondered where he was going.

'Hey little one,' one of the big horses said, trying to get Jacks attention, 'you'll get hurt if you don't get off the road.'

Jack was nervous and trotted on as quickly as he could until he heard a strange sound ahead of him. As he rounded a bend in the road he was confronted by a monster. What was this growling beast in front of him with smoke billowing from its feet? Although Jack had seen and heard cars passing by his old paddock, this was frightening – the biggest monster he had ever seen.

Jack backed up and reared as he had never done before. He didn't take his eyes off the monster for a second and was getting ready to turn and run. The lorry driver had seen Jack at the last minute and slammed on his brakes causing the tyres to skid and smoke. The driver could see that the little horse was terrified and his scrawny appearance shocked him. He was delivering hay to a local farm and was used to being around horses and he had never seen such a sad and scared horse. He was determined to give the little horse as much help as he could.

He turned the engine off and slowly climbed down from the cab but by this time Jack had turned and was trotting in the opposite direction with one eye fixed on the lorry.

The horses that had tried to warn him were looking on anxiously.

Within two hundred yards Jack was shocked to see another smaller monster approaching him in the narrow road. He stopped and stood in the road looking back at the big monster and then at the small monster. He could see a man walking towards him and from the small monster a lady had emerged and she too was heading his way.

The lady had turned her car engine off. Luckily, she too was experienced around horses, this was a rural area and most people came into contact with horses regularly one way or another. Jack could sense that these people were different to those who he had been around since his miserable life had begun with Billy.

As they approached him he could hear them speaking and their voices were reassuring and not scalding as he was used to hearing.

'Come on boy, there's a good lad,' the lorry driver said as he approached Jack slowly. The lorry driver had grabbed some rope from his cab in the hope that he could use it as a temporary head collar.

Jack backed up and at the same time he could hear the lady trying to calm him down.

'There's a good lad come on,' she said as she too approached from the other side as gently as she could.

It was not unreasonable for Jack to be so nervous. He had only ever met one kind human, Atalia, everyone else had been mean. He decided to make his getaway again and trotted past the lady with ease, he was so determined to get away he was even prepared to pass the small monster but he picked up more speed this time. He was now so disorientated and confused that he didn't know which direction he was going in, he was just so glad to be free.

He trotted down the road as fast as he could and as he looked back he could see the people getting back into their monsters. He was unaware that blood was gushing from his legs and chest and making his normally white ankles look like pink socks.

He eventually came across an opening in a hedge and decided to go through it. He was now out of sight and heading off across another field, he was really frightened but glad to be on his own. The lorry driver had a good view over the hedges and could see him in the field. When he got close to the entrance of the field, he parked his lorry to form a barrier. The field had a good strong fence around it and some high bushes in places and appeared to have only one entrance, so he knew that Jack could not escape.

The lorry driver knew it would be futile to try to catch the little horse and as the lady arrived after turning her car around to see if she could assist, they discussed what options they had. The lady suggested calling the RSPCA but the lorry driver knew of a horse and pony sanctuary a few miles away and suggested that they should drive there in her car to arrange for the little horse to be collected by them.

They arrived at the sanctuary within ten minutes and spoke to the manager, Suzie, relaying what had happened. Within minutes an emergency plan had been put into action and a field officer and a horsebox were heading towards the field where, by this time, Jack had calmed down slightly and was eating some fresh grass wondering what to do next.

The rescue party arrived within twenty minutes of being alerted and it was agreed that they should link hands and slowly walk towards Jack trapping him in the corner of the field where they could get a head collar on him and take him to safety. They knew the little horse before them would be frightened and approached slowly and calmly.

The plan eventually worked but not before Jack had given them the slip several times. His rescuers were very experienced and patient and it was their calm and reassuring voices that eventually made Jack realise that these people were not going to hurt him. It was not an easy task to get Jack into the horsebox as he had only ever been in a trailer before, but on that occasion he was only eight months old. That journey had brought him to the misery from which he was now trying to escape. Understandably, he wasn't sure about getting in the horsebox, despite the soft voices from the nice people. He put up a bit of a fight.

Eventually, he told himself that it would be different this time. They put a soft band on his hind quarter and gently persuaded him. His strength was drained and even if he had wanted to kick out he couldn't have.

Although Jack was still frightened by what had happened from the moment he decided to escape the paddock and the treatment he received from Billy, he found the horsebox strangely reassuring.

The people who had just put him in the horsebox reminded him of Atalia.

II

THE SANCTUARY

It was starting to get dark by the time they got to the sanctuary so Suzie decided to put Jack in a nice warm stable and dress his wounds. The sanctuary was always very busy and the volunteers sometimes struggled to find enough space for all the horses and ponies that needed their help. However, Suzie always kept one stable available just for this sort of occasion.

Once Jack was comfortable, he was given a small hay net and water before they left him to rest. It would be important to assess him properly in the daylight and work out what sort of diet he should be put on. Karen and David, two of the sanctuary workers were asked if they would stay overnight and check on Jack just in case he became frightened with his new surroundings. They did not need to be asked twice and were only too pleased that they could help. Jack was greatly reassured by friendly faces and voices when he woke up in the night.

Jack settled into his new surroundings but his ears were twitching all night at the different sounds around him and raindrops falling on the tin roof were unfamiliar. He wasn't used to lying down on such a thick bed of straw, as he had never been in a stable like this before since being with his mother. When he was forced to lie down due to sheer exhaustion, or when his feet were too painful to stand on, it was usually in a muddy field and then he would have terrible trouble getting up again.

Karen and David checked on Jack throughout the night and were pleased to see that he was not too frightened and didn't appear to be in pain despite the fact that he was in a terrible state. Morning came and as the sun rose and the rain clouds moved away, the sanctuary started to come to life. People were coming and going with wheelbarrows, hay nets, buckets of water, stable bedding and all manner of things that he had not seen since he had been with his mother.

Suzie had been the first to come and see him. She spoke to Karen about something called a log book. Suzie always gave new rescue animals new names, because it was a new start for them. Jack was given the new name of Louis-Springer but it would not be long before he was known as Lou.

David and Karen made their way home, tired but happy that Lou had spent a good night in the stable without too much fuss, while Suzie took some pictures of Lou. She knew that it was important to take photographs of any injuries and his general condition in the event that they would be required for the prosecution of those who had inflicted such pain and suffering on this little horse.

Suzie arranged for a vet to visit and also arranged for a farrier to attend later that day to trim his hooves, which were very long, and made him stand and walk unnaturally.

Lou was finding it all very strange, he had been exposed to so many people in such a short space of time and it was clear to him that they were all very caring people and took a keen interest in him.

Suzie appointed Sharon to muck out Lou's stable and to gently wash his wounds with warm water in readiness for the vet's visit. Just like Karen and David, Sharon took an immediate liking to Lou and she could sense that despite what he had been through he was surprisingly placid. She had seen so many horses and ponies come to the sanctuary that had been poorly treated and it was unusual for them to be so calm. Their trust in humans had usually been totally destroyed and it could take months and sometimes years to rebuild that trust. With Lou, they presumed that he must be so used to pain that he didn't kick up a fuss about it.

Lou was starting to trust in humans again and it was people like Sharon that made the difference to him, she was kind and her voice was never sharp like Billy's.

The vet arrived at midday and although he had other ponies and horses to attend to, it was Lou who he was directed to first. The sanctuary workers and indeed the vets and farriers were used to seeing horses and ponies in extremely poor conditions and Lou was one of the worst cases they had ever seen. As soon as the vet saw Lou he knew this was going to be a long-term healing process and that it would be many, many months before Lou was on the road to recovery.

He gave Lou a thorough examination and found several serious conditions that were in need of treatment and further investigation once he was slightly stronger.

Given the scars on his body and legs, he had obviously been subjected to some form of abuse. The open wound on his chest was infected, so the vet treated it immediately. The vet gave Lou some injections to start the healing process and then spoke to Suzie about what Lou would need over the next few weeks, just to get him out of danger. It was clear that he would need continuous monitoring in these early stages.

Before the vet had arrived, Sharon did a good job and Lou was cleaner than he had been for a long time, although now that he was all cleaned up, his bony frame looked even smaller than it had before. The farrier arrived in the afternoon and within an hour Lou's hooves were trimmed and smooth, for the first time since he had been taken away from his mother.

Suzie was not at all surprised that no one came forward to claim ownership of Lou, as they would have been in serious trouble with the RSPCA if they had.

It wasn't Suzie's policy to track owners down as she was more interested in helping the animals to get better. There was a strong network of "horsey" people in the area and if anyone knew where Lou had come from then it would soon be reported to her.

Lou was kept in a stable away from other horses until his wounds started to heal, for fear that the infections would spread.

As his wounds got better, he was allowed out into the fields to mix with the other horses and get the exercise that all horses need.

This allowed Lou to find out how things worked at the sanctuary and before long he had made a couple of friends who had explained the rules.

'Now then, Lou,' said Cannon, a wise old Welsh Cob who had been at the sanctuary for seven years, 'Suzie will not tolerate any fighting, kicking or escaping from the main fields into the farmers' fields.'

Lou listened intently as Cannon explained how naughty horses would be put in a small field with a big fence around and they weren't allowed to mix with the other horses if they were caught fighting.

It was soon evident to Lou that this was a place that had a structured attitude to the wellbeing of horses and ponies and the animals needs were the number one priority.

He worked out what was expected of him and since it wasn't in his nature to be naughty, he was satisfied that he would be treated well.

He was put on a special diet to help him put on weight and as the next few weeks went on it was clear from the vets visits and tests that there were further problems.

Lou went lame and the vets diagnosed a swelling of his leg joints.

After a few weeks, Lou was put into a horsebox and taken to a specialist centre for a scan and further investigations, but the news was not good. The scan of his joints confirmed that Lou was suffering from a condition that would require treatment.

Surgery would be required to repair the damage and clean the leg joints.

It was evident by the way Lou was walking that he was in pain but he always showed his placid nature and to the untrained eye he looked fairly well despite being underweight. Surgery was therefore essential as soon as possible, which was going to cost over £4,000.

Although Suzie wanted to help Lou, the sanctuary was a charity and just didn't have that sort of money. But if Lou didn't have the surgery, the pain would have become too much for him. It was unthinkable for such a young horse with a bright future ahead of him to be put to sleep. In desperation, Suzie contacted the local newspaper who readily agreed to run Lou's story in the daily paper and appeal for help.

Suzie was astounded at the response the article attracted; cheques and letters of support poured into the sanctuary over the next few days and weeks. Little else got done in the office other than logging all the money in and writing thank-you letters to Lou's benefactors.

Some of the messages brought tears to the sanctuary workers' eyes, in particular there was a letter from a pensioner who wrote 'Not a vast sum I know, but it is truly from the heart'.

The sanctuary workers tried to explain what was happening to Lou, and that there were lots of people out there who wanted to help him. They really wanted him to know that there were kind people out there, but he was in so much pain that he couldn't really understand what was going on.

Such was the response that within a matter of two weeks the sanctuary raised over double the amount required for the operation and Lou was booked in for his operation at the specialist veterinary unit at Newmarket.

Lou was put in a horsebox to be taken to the veterinary unit. On the way there, he knew that he was going to have something done to him but he had no idea what.

He had become used to the shooting pains in his legs and if he had known that the operation was going to remove that pain he would have been excited at the prospect. Instead he again felt apprehensive but strangely satisfied that whatever it was that the kind people at the sanctuary had arranged, it was going to be to his benefit.

Lou had his operation and afterwards his legs were bandaged and felt sore, but a couple of days later, the shooting pains that he had become used to disappeared. The procedure went well, although the specialist informed Suzie that Lou had multiple problems and might need more operations in the future.

Suzie decided to adopt a positive and practical approach to Louis' future management and for now she was intent on taking the very best of care of this special and fortunate little horse. Lou could feel the love from people and he wondered what had made his previous master, Billy, so uncaring and cruel. When he was alone, he often tried to work out what he had done wrong to have been so mistreated by Billy.

Lou showed his appreciation for the love and care shown to him by all of the new people in his life by being cooperative and he knew how to make people feel good. He would often gently lower his head and rub it against the people who cared for him, he was never aggressive with people or the other horses around him.

Lou often thought about Scamp and missed having him around but he was happy that at least Scamp was cared for more than he was.

III

BOBBY

At the sanctuary, all of the other horses and ponies admired Lou, he had been through so much but never complained about it. Lou had a presence that many of the other horses and ponies lacked; he would hold his head high and take in all that was going on around him. He made friends with some of the other horses and ponies and before too long he had many friends who wanted to know his story. Suzie was curious about why the horses and ponies were suddenly becoming noisier with their neighing and snorting. Little did she know that Lou and the other horses and ponies were swapping their stories of how they had ended up at the sanctuary. Before Lou arrived at the sanctuary, none of the horses or ponies communicated with each other regularly as they were terrified that they would be in trouble with Suzie if they were caught. Lou explained to them that providing they kept their neighing and snorting to a reasonable level while they were in the stable area that she would never know they were talking to each other.

They weren't to know that Suzie and the staff loved to hear the horses neighing and snorting – it was when a horse was quiet that they worried.

It wasn't long before Lou knew all of the names of the horses and ponies at the sanctuary and when they were out in the vast fields, they would all get together and hold meetings to discuss their future. They all loved it at the sanctuary but every now and then a horse or pony would be chosen to go to a special school to be trained to be ridden or just found a new foster home. They had also found out that the sanctuary would always be there for them if things didn't work out at the foster homes that had been chosen for them. It wasn't often that horses or ponies found their way back to the sanctuary, because Suzie was very careful about re-homing the horses and made sure they were going to good owners.

They had heard that Shelley, the girl who trained them, was kind and never mistreated them and that they could have fun with her. Those horses had a good life. Shelley had worked at the sanctuary as a volunteer when she was younger and had taken a keen interest in horses. As she got older she helped out at a local riding school that backed and broke the horses and ponies in from the sanctuary. Once they were trained they could be rehoused and start another life. The riding school offered stabling and all the necessary feed and bedding free of charge in order to help the sanctuary. However, it could take anything from eight weeks to six months or even more to train and find a new home for a horse or pony and in some cases it was not possible to re-home them.

The sanctuary catered for all types of horses from different backgrounds such as abandoned horses where people just could not afford to keep them anymore to abused horses. There were all breeds including Cobs, Warmbloods, Gypsy Horses, and Hackneys, Trotters, Shetlands, Mules and all manner of other ponies.

Lou became good friends with lots of different breeds, but his best friend was a French Trotter called Bobby. They would often spend hours out in the fields just grazing and talking about their futures. Bobby's life had been less stressful than that of Lou's and he was much healthier and more confident. This confidence could sometimes be a bit boisterous and while he wasn't aggressive, he did like to bite and kick out. To Bobby it was just a game and he didn't know that it was his boisterous nature that meant he was taken to the sanctuary as a horse that couldn't be trained.

Lou and Bobby were about the same height and age and Bobby was only too pleased to pass on his knowledge and experience to Lou.

'I want to be a show jumper when I get older and have my own stable,' Bobby told Lou.

'It's OK here but they often put me in different stables when they bring me in from the field.'

'What's a show jumper, Bobby?' Lou asked innocently.

Bobby started laughing and he laughed so loud that Suzie thought something was wrong with one of the horses in the field. As she walked into the field she could see Bobby rolling around on the ground with Lou standing next to him with his head held low.

As Suzie approached Bobby he got up, composed himself and carried on grazing.

'Are you OK there boy?' Suzie said as she checked him over, she was concerned that he may have been stung or that he had colic or had hurt himself somehow. After satisfying herself that everything was OK she walked off somewhat bemused.

'Why were you laughing?' Lou asked with his chest out but feeling slightly embarrassed.

'I can see we will have to educate you,' came Bobby's reply.

The two friends carried on grazing and as Lou didn't know what he wanted to be when he got older he decided he'd better stay quiet in case Bobby started laughing again.

The two horses had great respect for each other, although there was a little bit of friendly rivalry. Lou had clearly had a bad start in life and had some catching up to do to be as smart as Bobby.

The two horses were approaching three and a half years of age and by this time Lou had put on weight and was starting to look fit and strong, although he needed a schooling programme to build up his muscle. Bobby had already been backed and fostered out although the lady who fostered him decided that he was too much for her and he was returned to the sanctuary shortly after.

As time went on more horses and ponies were leaving the sanctuary for new homes, which always brought a tear to Lou and Bobby's eyes. All of the horses and ponies formed a strong bond at the sanctuary and they knew that it was unlikely that they would meet up again.

By now it was early spring and Bobby and Louis were inseparable. They were known as the troublesome duo by the sanctuary staff as they could always be found charging around the fields together.

Bobby would chase Lou and try to bite him on the back of his legs, there was no intention to cause harm - it was just the boys having fun.

To see these two horses play fighting and rearing up was an extremely beautiful sight, it was obvious that they enjoyed each other's company.

Bobby had heard that he was going to be taken to the riding school to be re-schooled by Shelley and found a new home.
He was happy at the sanctuary, but as more and more horses and ponies came in it was inevitable that he would have to move on at some point.

'Lou it's confirmed, I will be going soon,' Bobby told Lou when they were grazing one sunny day. He had agonised about telling him as he knew how sad Lou would be, Bobby was unhappy about it too but he understood why he had to go.

'What do you mean going?' Lou raised his head and looked at Bobby.

'We can't stay here forever Lou; it's only fair that we make way for others isn't it?'

'I'm coming with you then,' Lou told Bobby.

'It's not that easy Lou, and it's down to Suzie not me'.

Lou was not very strong emotionally and as he lowered his head Bobby could see Lou's eyes starting to water.

Lou walked away slowly, he didn't want his best friend to see him crying and he spent the rest of the afternoon on his own remembering all the good times they had enjoyed together.

Lou soon realised that even though he felt very sad, he should enjoy the last few days that he would spend with Bobby and, as it turned out, those were the greatest days of all. Even Suzie and the staff at the sanctuary couldn't understand what had got into the two boys. They were charging around and having races from one end of the field to the other, almost every time Bobby would beat Lou but on the occasions when Lou won he felt great.

Little did Lou know that Bobby was being kind and letting his friend win. He didn't want to leave Lou feeling so low.

The day came when it was time for Bobby to leave and Suzie was unsure how to handle things. She didn't know whether to leave Lou in the field or bring him up to the yard while Bobby was being loaded into the horsebox. She knew that they were friends and she put herself in their position.

Would I want to see my friend off she asked herself. 'Yes,' was the answer and so it was that Lou and Bobby were put into a small paddock as close to the main gate as possible.

Shelley and Lyn had arrived from the riding school and eventually the time came for Bobby and another little pony called Holly to be loaded into the horsebox.

Suzie put a head collar on Bobby and led him from the paddock with Lou looking on. Bobby knew he had to behave despite not wanting to be parted from Lou and as he gave a last look at Lou he entered the horsebox with no fuss.

Lou and Bobby had talked about this moment and they knew it would be hard on them both.

I've got to be strong for Lou's sake Bobby told himself, despite the urge to start crying.

As the horsebox pulled out of the sanctuary gates, Lou gave out the deepest saddest neigh he could muster and he could hear Bobby neighing back. Lou was distraught and cantering on the spot, his neighing got louder and as the distant sound of Bobby's neighs faded away Lou calmed down and just hung his head low.

Suzie knew that Lou would miss Bobby and went over to console him; she was surprised to see tears rolling down Lou's cheeks. She had never really considered if horses cried or not, but now she knew.

For the next few weeks, Lou could not be consoled by any of the other horses or ponies, there was no other horse like Bobby at the sanctuary. Eventually Lou came to terms with his loss and carried on enjoying the summer days with the other horses and ponies.

Bobby in the meantime was enjoying his new surroundings and it was true, Shelley, the trainer was good fun and very gentle with her training techniques.

Bobby decided that he would not make it easy for her though in the hope that he might be sent back to the sanctuary to be with Lou. No such luck, if nothing else, Shelley was a real match for Bobby. Shelley was only five feet tall and weighed but little and it was always a battle of wits with her and Bobby. It wasn't long before Bobby realised that he would have to give in to her, although Shelley knew that she had a horse with a strong character on her hands.

Bobby had arrived at the riding school with one of his friends from the sanctuary called Holly. She was a little Welsh Cob and they spent most nights out in the field together. They would often talk about the other horses and ponies, but in particular they would talk about Lou.

IV

LOU'S NEW HOME

While Lou persevered with life in general, he always thought about Bobby and the fun that they had enjoyed together, and even if he had a great day in the fields with his other friends, it was when he was alone that he would think about Bobby.

Bobby would also think of his best friend but his happy new life with Shelley would help him take his mind off of his past.

It's amazing to think how two young horses can be so much in tune with each other, Shelley thought to herself. She had seen a look in Bobby and Lou's faces on the day that she and Lyn had collected Bobby. Shelley had studied horses in more ways than most people did; she looked into their souls and eventually developed an ability to connect with horses and ponies that very few people are capable of.

Shelley's work continued with Bobby and Holly and since Bobby was a much finer breed of horse he needed twice the amount of work than Holly.

Although he played her up, she had him behaving in a short space of time. Bobby loved it, he could behave as he was expected to which is what he enjoyed most, but then he could be naughty if he wanted too.

Bobby knew how to push his luck but he knew Shelley would never abuse him.

Bobby also knew that his time at Lyn's riding school would be short, all of the horses and ponies knew that after they were trained, they were found new homes. Three months had passed and the time came for Bobby to be fostered out so he decided to use the opportunity to be reunited with Lou. He thought that if he misbehaved then he would be returned to the sanctuary.

Shelley and Lyn had done everything by the book to train him, but now Bobby wasn't having any of it. He would buck, rear up and generally be difficult, which was completely out of character. The only thought on his mind now was being with Lou.

He knew not to kick Lyn and Shelley but his weight and power would see him through, or so he thought.

Bobby hadn't thought for a moment that Lyn and Shelley had more patience than he had counted on and eventually he gave in. He wanted to be a show jumper and he soon realised that if he allowed Shelley and Lyn to train him then he might be allowed to achieve his dreams.

After he started to cooperate, he found that he was being allowed more time in the school than the other horses and ponies and that they were looking at him in a very different way. When Bobby arrived at Lyn's riding school he thought that the other horses and ponies didn't like him as they stared at him but would suddenly look away when he caught them staring. He had never realised that he was so handsome and that his beauty struck all the mares and the geldings were jealous of him.

By the time Bobby had been trained to become a trusted horse to ride he was enjoying life so much that his past thoughts fell away. He never forgot Lou but he knew that his friend would end up in a nice place.

'Oh how I would love for Lou to be here with me now,' he often thought. Bobby could never work out why he and Lou had been separated but he knew he had to behave.

When Shelley had eventually trained Bobby to be cooperative with the people who cared for and loved him, he submitted to his fate.

Lyn, Suzie and Shelley discussed Bobby's future and if there was anyone experienced enough on their long list of potential fosterers who could take him on again.

There were plenty of potential fosterers who wanted young horses and ponies, but how many were capable of caring for them in a way that met the sanctuary's high standards. Bobby was no ordinary horse and would require regular handling, riding and schooling.

Shelley arrived at the stables in the morning to attend to Bobby and Holly just as Lyn was starting her early morning round of feeding and bringing the horses and ponies in from the fields.

'Hi Lyn,' Shelley said in her usual happy manner, 'I was thinking about Bobby last night and I've had an idea, why don't I take Bobby on?' Shelley looked at Lyn hoping for a positive response.

Lyn looked at Shelley and it was as much as she could do to stop herself from crying with happiness.

If there was anyone who she thought Bobby should be with it was Shelley.

'That sounds a good idea Shelley but we will need to speak to Suzie first.'

Lyn couldn't wait to call Suzie to tell her the good news and made an excuse to walk up to her house straight away.

It was without doubt that Shelley should foster Bobby, she had trained so many of the sanctuary horses and ponies that she was deemed to be an expert who knew just what Bobby needed.

'Hello,' Suzie said as she answered the phone. 'Hi, Suzie, it's Lyn here, I have some great news for you.'

Suzie could tell by Lyn's voice that this news was special.

'Oh great Lyn, tell me quick. I need some good news.'

'We have found the perfect person to take on Bobby,' said Lyn excitedly.

'Well I hope they have plenty of experience,' replied Suzie, 'You know what a handful he can be.'

'Oh yes, but I think Shelley is the best person for the job, wouldn't you say.'

After a few seconds of silence Suzie spoke, 'Oh how fantastic, Lyn, that news has definitely made my day, no not my day, my year.'

The two of them discussed what needed to be done and Lyn went back down to the stables to give Shelley the good news that she had been accepted to be Bobby's new fosterer. Shelley entered into a proper agreement with Suzie and decided to stable Bobby permanently at Lyn's riding school. As the weeks went by with Shelley and Bobby bonding and enjoying life, Suzie, Shelley and Lyn continued to find responsible fosterers for their charges.

***

Lou had been having some basic training at the sanctuary and despite his slight nervousness he was affectionate and accepted his care with complete cooperation.

It had been many months since Bobby left and just as Bobby thought about Lou, so did Lou think about Bobby.

Lou had befriended a little Cob called Solo who had arrived just after Bobby left; she helped him to cope with losing his best friend. Lou was always talking about Bobby and how much he had learnt from him.

He would describe how they had raced and played games together. Solo had unfortunately misunderstood Lou when he told her that he had lost his best friend and assumed that Lou was grieving.

'Bobby will be looking down on you,' she told Lou in a sympathetic voice.

'What do you mean looking down on me?' Lou replied sharply.

'He's in heaven Lou, that's where all good horses go.'

'Bobby isn't dead,' Lou told her in a grumpy voice. 'He's just gone.'

Lou ignored Solo for the rest of the day and started to believe that he would just be moved on to be trained and found a home with someone who didn't understand him.

It was unlike Lou to feel so low but it seemed to him that every time things were going well, something happened and he would be left alone again. He was scared too that he would end up with someone like Billy, or even worse.

Solo felt a little bit stupid and was quite upset that her friend was ignoring her; it was unlike Lou to sulk, especially with her.

On the following day when Lou was feeling at his lowest, Solo decided that she should try to cheer him up and apologise for her mistake.

'I'm sorry about yesterday, Lou, it was my fault that...' Before Solo could say another word Lou spoke.

'Solo, nothing is your fault, I should have been clearer about where Bobby had gone and it's me who should be apologising to you.'

The two friends grazed and groomed each other for the rest of the day and laughed at what had happened. By the afternoon they were best of friends again and Lou was starting to feel much better.

Later that afternoon Lou and Solo were brought into the stables.

'What's going on Solo?' Lou asked her. 'I think we are being moved,' she told him.

They were eventually led to the front paddock by the sanctuary car park and when that happened, they knew that it was their time to make space for more horses and ponies. They were apprehensive about where they were going to be taken, but they were ready for it.

'Whenever a horsebox arrived it was an exciting time for all the horses and ponies. Although their life was comfortable at the sanctuary, they knew that moving on would mean new challenges and hopefully they would have their own stable. They knew that life would be as good as their life at the sanctuary and that they could make new friends.

When the moment came, it wasn't Shelley and Lyn who collected them as Lou had hoped, but a tall man by the name of Graham, who was Lyn's husband and a shorter man called John.

Both Lou and Solo were loaded with ease and after a short ride to their new home they were put into stables away from the other horses and ponies to ensure that if they had any colds or other illnesses that they were remedied before mixing with the other horses. It was highly unlikely that Lou or Solo would have been allowed to come to Lyn's yard without being fully fit but Lyn always implemented quarantine regulations to ensure the health of her riding school horses and ponies and the other liveries.

After two weeks of separation and monitoring it was clear that Lou and Solo were healthy. Shelley knew that Lou was in the yard and it burned her heart that she couldn't put Bobby and Lou in the field together. Lyn also knew that Bobby and Lou had been best of friends but she also knew that she had to follow the rules – new horses couldn't mix with the others until they had been quarantined. Finally they were moved closer to some of the other horses. Solo had managed to ask another horse if there were any of the sanctuary horses at the yard and she heard Bobby's name mentioned. She told Lou and although she wasn't completely sure it was his friend, he could sense that Bobby was there.

Lou wanted to let Bobby know that he was there, but he also wanted to surprise him. If Solo was right then this would be a very special moment for them all.

Lyn and Shelley met for their usual morning meeting the next day and it made Shelley's eyes fill up with tears when Lyn told her that Bobby and Lou could now be reunited.

'Oh my god,' Shelley said, she had been looking forward to this moment. How would the two friends behave she asked herself. Shelley put a head collar on Lou and led him around to the part of the yard where Bobby was stabled.

As the two friends spotted each other their ears pricked up and they stood tall.

The noise was deafening, the two young horses were neighing and Lou was bouncing up and down on his front legs. All of the other horses and ponies looked on and were puzzled at the scene unfolding in front of them. Bobby was circling in his stable and repeatedly looking out at Lou each time his head reached the stable door opening; it was as if he was imagining things and that any moment Lou would be gone.

Shelley tied Lou up at the rail and then brought Bobby out of the stable. She tied Bobby up next to Lou and the two boys were soon rubbing their heads on each other.

'Bobby, it's you, I can't believe it!' Lou was beside himself. Although he was fairly sure about Bobby being there and that they would be together again, he had convinced himself while he was at the sanctuary that he would never see Bobby again.

Bobby had no idea that Lou had been there for two weeks and was really happy.

The scene brought a tear to Shelley's eyes, and it brought memories racing back to her of giving her dad a hug when he came back from one of his six-month stints in the Middle East. She fully remembered the moment when he walked through the door so she knew how the two friends felt.

Bobby was put in a large field with Lou and Solo. Shelley and Lyn had led them down to the field and, apart from a little horseplay from Bobby, things seemed normal.

As soon as the boys got into the field it was a sight to behold. Lou had been holding himself back until this moment. They ran down the field like two old friends who ran together every day.

The two boys got up to their old tricks and within ten minutes they were play fighting and chasing each other around the field.

Solo now realised why Lou had been so upset, they were the best of friends and that was clear. She felt slightly left out and there was no way that she could keep up with the boys.

Eventually when they had calmed down, Lou realised that he should introduce Bobby to Solo.

'This is Bobby,' he told her. 'Didn't I tell you how good looking he was?'

'Well he's not bad Lou, but you are just as handsome you know.' Lou blushed and walked away while Bobby and Solo became acquainted.

'He missed you so much you know Bobby; he never stops talking about you.'

'I don't doubt you Solo, we had so much fun and when I had to leave it broke my heart too.'

The three of them spent a peaceful afternoon and night in the field and chatted about their plans for the future. Bobby explained to both of them how things worked at Lyn's yard and what they could expect. He told them about Shelley and how she had fostered him and told them that he now lived at the riding school.

Never had three horses spent such a fantastic night together in a moonlit field.

V

JOHN MEETS LOU

Shelley and Lyn collected the three horses from the field in the morning; Lou and Solo were put in little paddocks with their own temporary stables while Bobby went back to his own stable, which was fitted out with rug holders and a little tack room that Shelley's dad had built for her.

Shelley rode Bobby most days of the week so he was very fit and his chestnut coat was shiny like silk. Lou had noticed that his friend had looked much fitter and he was quite jealous.

'I wonder if I will ever be like Bobby,' he had said to Solo across the fence that morning. 'Have you seen the muscles on his legs and neck?'

'Of course you will Lou, I'm sure Shelley will put you through the same training and have your muscles rippling just like Bobby's.'

'Thanks Solo, you always say the right things.'

Solo was so glad to be stabled next to Lou, she was a bit shy and found it hard to make friends. They couldn't see Bobby's stable from where they were but every now and then they could hear him neighing and they would both reply as loud as they could.

Shelley took Bobby out for his daily ride and had planned to start work on Lou just as soon as she got back.

Bobby knew that Lou was nervous about his training and as Shelley returned from her ride and rode him down the long driveway to the riding stable he neighed loud enough to ensure that Lou knew he was back.

Lou heard Bobby and replied, within minutes Bobby had been un-tacked and put in his stable with a newly filled hay net and a stable rug on to stop him getting cold.

Shelley and Lyn prepared the equipment that they would need to start to introduce Lou to the methods that are used to exercise horses called longeing, which required them to connect a long rope to a cavesson, which is similar to a head collar but with metal rings on the top of the nose band to connect a longe rope to. The trainers would then hold the rope gently to guide horses through their exercise.

They collected Lou from the stable in his normal head collar and took him into the undercover school.

They put the cavesson on him, which he noticed was different to anything that he had seen before, but Shelley was so gentle with him that he had no reason to fear anything.

Lyn connected the longe rope to one of the rings on top of the cavesson and within a short time he was walking and trotting for her as she required.

He knew what to do instinctively and such was his strength and power that he was only too pleased to be flexing his muscles.

For the next few days Lou had the same type of training and though it was becoming more tiring he thoroughly enjoyed it.

'Oh Solo, it's so nice to get out of the stable and exercise. I love it.'

Solo was quite happy to spend her time grazing and wandering around the field. She knew her time would come to be trained. Lou and Bobby were very different types of horses to her; she knew that they needed to gallop and have more exercise than her.

After some initial training, which included Shelley laying across Lou's back with Lyn holding the head collar, it was time for Shelley and Lyn to introduce Lou to having a saddle on his back.

They proceeded to carry out their well-versed training procedures and Lou accepted the saddle being placed on him with the girth strap fastened very loosely, although he did flinch slightly.

He felt confident that Shelley and Lyn were never going to hurt him.

Shelley noticed that Lou would flinch more when she touched his right-hand side and it was clear to her that it was the side where he was whipped.

Lou had more training with the saddle and soon became used to it, enjoying it more and more as the days went on.

Shelley and Lyn knew that they would need to be patient with Lou, he had been through so much at a young age and things could not be rushed.

The time came for Shelley and Lyn to introduce Lou to having a rider on his back, the process was straight forward enough but every horse reacted differently.

Lou remembered what Bobby had told him about the training, and the trust he had in Bobby was never going to be in question.

Lou was led into a stable where straw bales were placed around the edges for protection just in case Lou unexpectedly bucked off his rider.

Lyn held on to the bridle and gently stroked Lou on the neck to try to assure him that everything was OK while Shelley stood on the two straw bales that she would use to get up to the height that she would need to gently lie across the saddle.

As she put her weight onto the saddle Lou's muscles flinched at first and then his whole body went stiff.

Bobby had told him not to be worried about being ridden but he also told him that it was a very strange and unnatural feeling at first.

After a little fidgeting and trying to move away from the left-hand side where Shelley had laid across the saddle he relaxed slightly and realised that it wasn't so bad after all.

Shelley was really happy that Lou hadn't reared and bucked as some horses had done before.

She lowered herself down gently from the saddle and they turned Lou around and tried the same on the opposite side but this was going to be very different. When Lou was rescued he had several scars on his body and in particular on his right hand hindquarter, so as Shelley tried to put weight on his right-hand side he started to panic.

Shelley knew from grooming Lou that he was still fragile and that although his scars had healed, the mental pain was still there. Shelley and Lyn knew that they needed to end the training there and then; they knew that Lou would need to be trained very slowly.

***

Over the next few weeks Shelley and Lyn increased the process and Lou became satisfied that he had nothing to worry about. It wasn't long before Shelley was in the saddle and walking and trotting him around the indoor school.

Shelley's dad, John, often arranged to go riding with her on Shannon, one of Lyn's riding school horses; he had ridden for many years and had taken a keen interest in both Bobby and Lou's progress.

'So how is Lou coming along Shelley?' he asked his daughter on one of his visits.

'He's really coming on well Dad; he's got such a placid nature.'

John had not considered taking on a horse but there was something about Lou that intrigued him; he had heard about the life that Lou had come from and was amazed at how he was turning out.

'How long will it be before he's ready to be fostered Shelley?'

'Oh I think it will be at least another two or three months before he's ready Dad'. Shelley was curious about why her dad was taking such an interest but then he always took an interest in her life.

'There are a couple of people interested in him who have experience with horses so I don't think we will have a problem finding a responsible fosterer for him,' she told him.

John had decided that he would take more interest in Lou and with any luck he would be able to foster him, but he knew he would have to prove his sincerity first.

'What about if I were to apply to the sanctuary to be his fosterer Shelley?'

'Oh, Dad that would be great, but he will need lots of attention and further schooling.'

John had enjoyed many years of simple riding out with friends but he was a novice rider and had never had his own horse, so he was very apprehensive but excited about taking on Lou.

Shelley was excited about the possibility of riding out on Bobby with her dad on Lou and hoped that he was really serious.

John thought about his proposal and as Shelley had advised him to write a formal letter to the sanctuary sooner rather than later, that's exactly what he did. He composed a letter and sent it in with the formal application the following day, as he was worried that someone else may beat him to it.

Dear Suzie

Re: Horse Fostering Programme

Please find herewith my completed application for fostering a horse.

I am fortunate enough to be Shelley's father and I have seen many of the horses and ponies that she has painstakingly trained to a very good standard in order for them to be fostered.

Shelley has inspired me to become a more accomplished rider and take on the commitment of giving a rescue horse a good home. Bobby is just one of her most successfully trained horses and this has really made me proud of her accomplishments.

Although I am an accomplished rider and have ridden for many years on and off, I will be entering into a refresher programme to bring myself up to a better standard to take on the challenges of a young horse.

I have had the privilege of seeing Shelley train Louis-Springer and although there is still work to do, I feel that Louis would be very suitable for me if I were successful in becoming a horse fosterer.

I very much look forward to seeing Louis progress and hope that my application is successful.

Kind Regards

John Sales

John hoped that the endorsement on the formal application from Shelley and Lyn would go a long way to him being successful.

Although others had expressed an interest in Lou they had not made a formal application so after an interview with Suzie she accepted his application.

She was so pleased as she knew that John would have the support of Shelley and that Lou would be in the very best hands.

***

Over the next couple of months Lou came on leaps and bounds and as Shelley and Lyn introduced him to riding out on public roads and bridleways, they were moved at how he seemed to enjoy it, despite his nervousness of the monsters he met such as trucks, buses and lorries.

Lyn would ride Bobby while Shelley rode Lou, and despite some initial nervousness, Lou soon gained trust with his rider's confidence.

This was in no small part to the constant support of his best friend Bobby.

'Well done, Lou,' Bobby would say encouragingly to him when they were out in the snow-covered fields. 'You looked fantastic trotting up the road and did you see the way that people were looking and admiring you?'

Lou blushed and knew his friend was being overly complementary to boost his confidence, which had the desired effect.

When Bobby and Lou were out in the fields at night and whenever they were together Bobby complimented Lou on how he was improving on his riding skills and in particular Bobby had told Lou how his riders respected him.

Shelley invited her dad up to see some of the horses that she was training and introduced him to Lou. John was always interested in what she was doing and loved to help out in any way he could, especially if it involved befriending Lou. He started to help with grooming Lou and taking him back to the stable after his rides out with Shelley and Lyn.

John loved bringing treats to Lou and would always turn up with fresh apples and carrots, but although he would treat all of the other horses to similar treats, Lou always got a little bit more.

Lou liked John, but he could see that he was not experienced in grooming or cleaning out his hooves, but he was gentle and Lou responded to this kind treatment by being cooperative. He had no reason to be difficult with John and a bond was starting to develop between them both.

'Lou is a beautiful horse Shelley, he is so gentle given the experience that he's been through,' John told his daughter.

Shelley had previously told her dad about how Lou was found and what he had been through and although John had not seen Lou in his poor state, he could only imagine what Lou's ordeal had been like.

***

'Lou,' said Bobby, 'I know you are nervous about the training and all the different things that we have to learn, but trust me, Shelley doesn't do anything that will make you look silly and she will never expect you to do things that you are not capable of'.

As always Lou listened to Bobby's wise words of wisdom and took everything in.

Shelley eventually started to take Lou out without Bobby, which was part of the usual training to get the horses more confident about being out on their own. He was becoming accustomed to the traffic on the odd occasion when they had to travel on the road. Part of his training over the past couple of months involved him being walked down back roads with Shelley on him. He had been nervous when cars approached, but as usual he was a quick learner and coped well. He had now learnt to trot and canter with the appropriate commands and loved to be out riding in the open fields with Shelley.

As John had been attending the stables regularly to see Lou being put through his planned training, eventually Shelley decided to put her dad on Lou.

Lou had seen John on many occasions and although John had groomed him from time to time, Lou was naturally nervous.

'OK, come on Dad its time you got on Lou; let's see how you two get along.'

John was slightly nervous as he tacked Lou up and led him into the school. Shelley decided to ride Lou first, just to get him warmed up and to get a little bit of energy out of him, he was a powerful horse and she wasn't quite sure how he would cope with the increased weight of her dad.

John weighed about three stone more than Shelley and Lou had only ever been ridden by Shelley so he was bound to notice the difference

After ten minutes of walking and trotting on Lou, Shelley dismounted and led him over to the mounting block where John was nervously waiting. He had ridden many Cobs but to ride a Hackney was a very different proposition - Cobs are a much wider breed of horse and as soon as John put his weight on Lou he realised the difference in the seating position. Lou stood motionless while John gently put his foot in the stirrup and as he put his full weight in to it and lifted his leg over the saddle, Lou could feel that something was different.

He visibly went stiff and looked at Shelley as if to say: 'what's happening, why are you there and not on my back?'

John sat there for a moment while Lou adjusted himself to this extra weight and Shelley adjusted the girth.

'OK, Dad just walk him round for now. I want him to get used to the extra weight today before we try anything else.'

John walked him round and with Shelley advising him on what to do, he could immediately understand that Lou needed only the slightest of commands as he was very responsive.

After twenty minutes John decided to dismount and take Lou back to have the saddle and bridle removed and have his cooler rug put on to absorb the sweat that Lou had produced.

It was important for Lou and John that they take things slowly at first so as not to tire Lou out. As John dismounted he caught his right leg on Lou's hind quarter very gently which made Lou flinch quite abruptly.

'Dad you need to be careful, he's still a bit nervous about being touched on his back but he will soon be over it, hopefully.'

John felt disappointed that he had ended up by making Lou flinch and he knew that he had much to learn about this special horse.

John walked back to the stable area and tied Lou up to un-tack him. He was quite surprised that his legs felt like jelly.

'Sitting on Lou was strange,' he told Shelley, 'It's like sitting on a fence compared to the big wide Cobs that I am used to riding.'

Shelley laughed, 'you'd better get used to it, Dad, he won't get much wider.'

Shelley and Lyn had one of their usual meetings to discuss the workload and whether they could take on more horses from the sanctuary in the coming weeks.

Shelley had trained Solo by this time and she had been found a new home much to Lou's disappointment, he had been so preoccupied with his own training that he almost forgot that Solo would probably be found a new home.

On the day before Solo was to be moved Lyn had put her and the boys in the field for the night so that they could say their goodbyes. She wasn't sure if horses communicated in the same way as humans but she was sure they had emotions and wanted Solo to spend her last night there with her friends.

'Well, Solo, you take care out there,' Bobby said just to break the ice; he could see that she was feeling low and wouldn't leave Lou's side.

'That's right, Solo,' said Lou. 'You will have your own stable and be spoilt, there's no doubt about that'.

Solo had accepted that she would be moved on before Lou as Cobs were so much easier to train due to their calm demeanour but that didn't help, she was going to miss him more than anything else. Bobby wandered off and left Lou and Solo to spend some time on their own, he knew just how close they were.

When they were brought in from the field in the morning and fed, Solo was loaded into the horsebox to be moved to her new home. Bobby and Lou looked on with pride; they had helped her to become more confident and knew she would be loved as they loved her. Just as Lou had been advised and mentored by Bobby, so had Solo. He had treated her kindly and had warned her that there are horses who played very roughly and that she should avoid situations where larger horses play fight.

'Bigger horses don't realise what damage they can do to smaller horses,' he told her, 'and although it's good to run with the pack, you need to run with horses your own size,'.

As the horsebox slowly pulled out of the driveway, all of the horses and ponies were neighing and letting her know that she would be missed. Tears streaked down her face but as Bobby and Lou had told her, it was only to make way for another sanctuary horse or pony which made her feel slightly better. She knew there were lots of horses that needed helping.

Bobby and Lou went to their hay nets and hid their faces, they were both crying but they didn't want the others to see them.

VI

A NEW HOME FOR LOU

It was early spring and John spent more and more time at the stables grooming Lou and riding him out with Shelley on the local roads and bridle paths.

Lou could feel the respect that John gave him and responded equally. John had always been careful when grooming horses and knew the power that they had in their back legs should they decide to kick out.

Shelley had told him to be careful when picking the mud out of Lou's hooves and although Lou had never kicked anyone, it was always possible that he could kick out if the hoof pick was being handled wrongly causing a sharp pain in the horses foot.

The two were becoming used to each other, John visited the local saddlery or 'horse heaven' as Shelley nicknamed it, to buy all of the equipment that would be needed for the day when Lou became his sole responsibility.

Lou was approaching his fifth birthday and due to his operation and subsequent rehabilitation it was a later age than normal for him to be ready to be ridden.

John and Shelley loved to put Bobby and Lou in the field together, they would spend fifteen to twenty minutes chasing each other around the field before settling down to graze on the fresh grass.

Both Lou and Bobby loved these times together and to them life was fantastic. They had lovely conditions, good grazing and seemed to be treated like special horses at Lyn's yard.

John found a riding stable close to where he lived. The facilities were great, with an outdoor school and plenty of surrounding fields that were well managed to provide all year round turnout. The fields had fencing whereby areas could be rested so that new grass could grow in one field while the horses chomped on the grass in the others.

The riding school owner was more than happy to offer Lou a stable there and it suited John as they offered assisted livery at a reasonable cost. This meant that Lou would be well looked after while John was at work. John would only have to bring Lou in from the field in the afternoon when he had finished work, as the stable staff could give Lou his breakfast and put him out in the field in the morning.

The stable staff would also muck out the stable during the day, fill the water container and keep an eye out for Lou to make sure he was enjoying the wide open fields in which he would have the freedom to roam.

There was no doubt that the sanctuary field officer would find this place acceptable and the day after the visit was carried out John had confirmation that everything had been accepted and passed as fit for Lou's welfare.

As the day approached when Lou would be moved to his new stables, Shelley became concerned about Lou's move away from Bobby and wondered just how the two friends would react.

Lou had heard John and Shelley talking about his imminent move and he knew he had to tell Bobby.

'Well, Bobby, we better make the most of the next few days as I'm going to be moved next week.'

Bobby was used to the coming and going of horses and ponies that he had befriended but being parted from Lou once again did make him feel quite upset. He knew that Lou would not want him to show how he felt about it and tried to act as normal, but it was far from how he really felt.

The spring was turning into summer and the days were bright and sunny so they really did have some fun.

'Come on, Lou I'll give you a race across the field,' Bobby said as they were put out in the field that day.

Lyn and Shelley were bemused, they had seen the two friends have much fun over the past few months but today was something different.

They were racing and bucking, leaping and neighing like never before, and the next few days were just the same.

Everything was made ready for Lou at his new stable and John was getting excited about his new found responsibilities and change of lifestyle. John was a well-respected writer for the transport industry and his work commitments took him to various places around the country but he knew that his priorities would have to change and that Lou would require his full attention.

Preparations were made for Lou to be transported the six miles to his new stables and Natasha the stable owner agreed that Shelley could bring Bobby there for a couple of days to help Lou settle in.

Shelley didn't want to see the two friends parted yet again, but it was not possible for Lou to remain at Lyn's stables. Apart from a few liveries, there were Lyn's riding school horses and ponies and she always had to have a stable for the sanctuary horses.

On the day when Lou was to be moved, the two horses were loaded into the horsebox, they were confused at what was happening

Although Lou knew that he was going to a new home with John, who he had come to respect and had bonded with, he was unsure what to think when Bobby was loaded into the horsebox with him.

'Oh Bobby, that's great,' said Lou when they were in the horsebox, 'we're both going to the new stable.'

'Are you sure, Lou?' Bobby said somewhat confused; he knew that Shelley worked at the riding stable most days, training the new horses and ponies, so it wouldn't make sense for him to be moved.

'Well why are we both going then?' said Lou just as confused as Bobby.

They arrived at the new stable where Natasha was waiting to meet them with John. She had prepared two stables next to each other and had arranged for Tiffany, one of the full time grooms, to accompany Shelley and John on a ride out on the following day to show them the area.

The horses were fed and stabled for the night while Shelley and her dad went off, happy in the knowledge that Lou and Bobby were settled.

The following morning after the horses had been fed and the stables mucked out, Tiffany brought her horse, Camilla, around to the rail to be groomed and tacked up.

'Oh my god, I don't believe it,' exclaimed Shelley as she held her mouth looking at Camilla. 'Please tell me that's who I think it is,' she said as she looked up at the most beautiful Dutch Warm Blood she had ever seen.

Tiffany was confused, 'This is Camilla,' she said as she looked at Shelley who seemed to be in shock.

'I remember working with her at the sanctuary and then re-breaking her at Lyn's, she is gorgeous now.'

As Shelley approached Camilla it was clear that she recognised Shelley. Camilla raised her head and snorted and continued to nod for what seemed like several minutes to Shelley. Never shy, she struck a couple of poses to show off her glossy chestnut coat.

A tear crept out of Shelley's eye and Camilla too grew watery-eyed. It wasn't often that Shelley bumped into the horses that she had painstakingly spent hours grooming, training and then having to say goodbye to. She explained things to Tiffany who was equally emotional, she loved her horse and it was a privilege for her to meet Camilla's original trainer.

'Wow! Who's that?' Bobby said to Lou as he was looking at Camilla.

'I don't know,' said Lou 'but she sure is a fine looking mare.'

After they were groomed the horses were tacked up and they were on their way down the lanes.

The immediate area was very flat and the roads were quiet and lined with tall hedges, 'the riders could see over the top of, where cows and sheep were grazing in the fields.

'Oh, Dad, its lovely here, Lou's going to love it.'

'You wait until we get to the woods,' Tiffany said with an air of excitement. They could see some woodland rising up steeply about a mile ahead just across a meadow. The trees were starting to come into bud and they could see that they were very dense.

Tiffany led the way and before too long they were at the bottom of the line of trees and entering a narrow but well-kept bridle path.

'Do you want me to lead?' Tiffany asked politely. 'There are various ways we can go and the bridle path forks off in different directions; if you don't know the woods it's easy to lose your way.'

'Yes, I think that would be best,' said Shelley very excited about the unfamiliar woods.

Bobby had been to various woods with Shelley and the environment was not too imposing to him, but Lou had only been to some small flat wooded areas so this was something very much out of his comfort zone.

Lou looked at Bobby with a concerned look on his face. He could see that the woods rose upwards and as they left the open bridle path it seemed to Lou as if a curtain had been drawn and the sun had been obscured by the trees.

'Don't worry, Lou,' said Bobby who could see the trepidation on Lou's face. 'You just need to look straight ahead and beware of the overhanging branches. It will be a good ride I'm sure'.

The usual advice from Bobby was enough to give Lou the extra confidence he so needed.

'Dad, you ride behind Tiffany and just let me know if you have any problems.'

Shelley had already told Tiffany that Lou had only recently been broken in and that she should take it easy.

'I'll start off with a steady trot,' said Tiffany 'then if you're happy we'll pick it up to a canter on the straights, if that's OK with you.'

'That's fine, John replied rather nervously.'

Although he was a confident rider he hadn't done much cantering on Lou and as he was used to riding Cobs; he already knew that Lou was a very different ride altogether.

The three of them trotted for about five minutes as the bridle path wound its way up through the woods.

As they reached the top of the hill and slowed to a walk there was an opening where they could look back down over the area they had covered, the scenery was stunning.

The sun was shining over the fields and they could see cattle grazing and the early shoots of crops starting to rise through the earth.

The fields looked like a patchwork quilt of greens and browns, mixed with the early yellow spikes of corn.

'OK the path widens up now,' said Tiffany 'and it is fairly straight so we can canter now if you're ready, but just beware there are two forks in the path and I will be taking the left fork each time.'

Lou was keeping up with Camilla with ease but he was very apprehensive and would often turn his head to get a reassuring look from Bobby, who was watching his friend with pride.

Bobby knew how Lou would be feeling and was so pleased to be out with him on one of his first major riding experiences.

'OK Tiffany that's fine,' said Shelley. 'Are you ready, Dad?'

'Yes, I'm ready, Shelley,' John said as he prepared his reins and set his feet firmly in his stirrups.

Tiffany trotted on and then very quickly picked Camilla up to a steady canter; Lou and Bobby hardly needed any commands, they were only too happy to get going.

Both Lou and John felt that their new relationship was being put to the test and despite the fact that they were both very nervous, their confidence was growing for each other by the second.

John knew that Lou could feel his slight commands and Lou responded to them as though the two of them had been riding together for years.

The bridle path was very flat and although it wound through the woods on the ridge of the hill, the turns were slow and there were no overhanging branches.

The first fork in the path was fairly sharp, but it was easy to see that the way was clear; the path narrowed and rose up again before reaching the top.

At the top of the hill Tiffany had increased the canter slightly, looking back from time to time to make sure things were OK.

John's heart was pounding, the exhilaration was incredible; he had two very experienced riders with him, which gave him the confidence he needed.

'Are you OK Dad?' yelled Shelley as they cantered along.

'Yeah I'm fine,' was all John could manage, such was his concentration.

At the top of the hill the second fork turned quite abruptly and Tiffany slowed down to a fast trot in order to avoid any mishaps.

The path widened again and started down the hill, which was very gradual and clear. The three of them slowed to a steady trot once again and then to a walk, it was obvious that all three horses were enjoying it.

As they reached the bottom of the hill, the path wound round to the left and levelled out; Tiffany brought them to a halt.

They had completed a popular circuit of one part of the woods and were back at the narrow path where they had entered.

'That was fantastic, Tiffany, you must love coming up here,' said Shelley with a huge grin on her face.

'I do enjoy it and try to come up here and the other woods at least twice a week,' Tiffany replied.

'Dad, I am so envious of you, the riding is so much better here than where I am.'

John was just glad to be still, although he had enjoyed the ride immensely he felt very elated, this was the longest ride

he had been on with Lou and the twists and turns, although very slight did unnerve him.

As they made their way back to the stables Lou looked casually around at the surrounding area, he felt as if he'd been there before, but he just dismissed it and thought no more of it.

When the horses had been un-tacked and sponged down, they were put in their stables with fresh hay nets and a few treats.

John always had a pack of mints in his pocket and would treat Lou and Bobby after a ride or after they had been groomed.

Lou was quite patient and would wait until the mints were offered, but once Bobby knew there were treats he would force his head into John's side trying to steal the whole pack.

The two horses were made comfortable for the night while Shelley and her dad went home for dinner and to discuss how the day went and what they were going to do the following day.

'Oh Dad, I'm so proud of you,' said Shelley. 'I would never have believed we would be riding our own horses out together six months ago.' John was so proud of Shelley and all that she had done for the rescue horses and was so glad to be a part of it.

'All I can say Shelley is that had it not been for you and Lyn, Lou and I would not be a couple today.' This made them both laugh and they spent the next couple of hours talking over the ride they had been on and how well behaved the horses had been. In particular they were so complimentary about Lou, who was the least experienced of the three horses.

'I think we should do the same ride tomorrow but in the opposite direction,' Shelley suggested.

'That suits me, Shelley, and perhaps we can check out one of the other paths for a shorter route, I'm not always going to have time for a long ride.

The next day was to be the last that Lou would spend with Bobby for a while although neither of them knew it.

'Hey, Bobby, when we were out today, I was sure that I'd been there before,' said Lou that evening as they were looking out of their stable doors at the unfamiliar yard.

'What makes you say that, Lou?' replied Bobby.

'I don't know really, but it was a strong feeling rather than anything that I saw.' Lou felt a bit silly but it was a strange feeling that he had experienced and as Bobby had always given him good advice, he thought he should know.

'It's probably nothing,' he said before lying down on the freshly made bed.

'Those country roads looked the same to me Lou,' said Bobby trying to support his friend. Bobby could hear the concern in Lou's voice, but was sure that it was nothing to worry about.

The following morning Shelley and John arrived to feed the horses and muck out the stables.

After being fed, Lou and Bobby were taken to one of the small fields for an hour to stretch their legs before being prepared for the ride.

Tiffany arrived and asked if they would like to join her on a ride to a different wood to the one they had visited the day before. After a brief chat it was agreed that they would take a new route as suggested by Tiffany, since she knew the area so much better, and they decided to go by road and visit a larger and hillier wood.

A short time later all three horses were tacked up and ready to go, Tiffany once again took the lead with John in the middle and Shelley at the rear.

Lou had forgotten about his strange feeling on the ride the day before and after seeing Bobby and Camilla he was looking forward to riding out again with John on his back.

The road twisted and turned with hedges on either side but, being so high up, the riders could easily see any cars approaching and their hi-visibility tops warned the oncoming cars to slow down.

As they rounded a small bend in the road they passed a house on the right-hand side. To the left was a small paddock with high hedgerows to both sides and a wooden fence to the front. There was another wooden fence and a shoddily built stable at the rear and in the middle of the paddock was a wide oak tree.

On the driveway to the house was a white truck and an old horse trap.

Although there had been some changes, Lou recognised the paddock immediately, his whole body shuddered instinctively as his ears pricked up and he was looking all around as if he was expecting to see something nasty.

'Whoa Lou,' said John trying to calm him down, 'What's the matter boy?'

Shelley was behind and saw what had happened, she too was baffled by Lou's behaviour.

Bobby spotted Lou's behaviour and it was something that only horses could sense that made him feel quite concerned for his friend.

Bobby knew Lou so well that he understood more than John or Shelley would ever know that Lou had experienced something that they could not understand.

'Just leg him on gently, Dad' Shelley said encouragingly, John did as he was told and Lou didn't need a second reminder, he passed Tiffany and Camilla at a fast trot.

When they had passed the house and the oak tree that Lou had spent many hours cowering under in torrential rain, he knew he would need to relay to Bobby what had happened to him in that paddock.

Lou had managed to suppress his past and had never believed for one minute that he would end up being so close to that awful place again.

Tiffany had seen Lou's reaction to the paddock that they had passed and although she didn't know what Lou was really frightened of, she decided to take them through the woods and return on a different lane.

The ride was good and Lou soon relaxed when they were trotting and cantering up the flat and wide bridle paths in the woods that Tiffany had chosen.

They returned to the stables via the bridle path and quiet roads where all appeared normal, except to Lou and Bobby.

'What happened back there when we were on the ride out?' asked Tiffany.

'I'm not sure,' said Shelley. 'I think Lou must have spooked at something, maybe the white truck in the driveway or something that we didn't see.'

The girls put it down to just normal horse nerves, which can often be found in young horses.

That evening when the horses had been stabled, Lou and Bobby overheard Shelley telling Tiffany that she would be taking Bobby back home and that it was their last night for a while before they would be together again.

'Bobby,' said Lou, when he knew there were no other horses to hear him 'You know when we passed that house with the oak tree and the truck, that's where I was before I escaped and was rescued by Suzie.'

Although Bobby was a bit more experienced than Lou with riding and being around other horses he also knew that he should be careful with his answers.

'Well, you are here now Lou, so you need to forget about the past.'

'But I can't, Bobby, if those people treated me so cruelly then they will treat all horses the same, won't they?'

Although Lou hadn't seen another horse in the paddock, he was concerned that someday another horse might be treated the same way as he was in that awful place.

Bobby thought about what Lou had said and although he hadn't experienced the torment that Lou had been through, he knew that Lou was right.

'You're right, Lou, and I'll tell you what we will do about it.'

Lou was so glad he had shared his secret with his best friend. Bobby had a plan and that night the two friends discussed exactly what they would do. They knew they would be seeing each other again as they had overheard Shelley and her dad agreeing to ride together as often as they could.

It would mean that Lou or Bobby would need to be moved by horsebox or trailer in order for them to be together but they were prepared for that.

VII

BILLY

The following morning the horsebox arrived to take Bobby back to Lyn's yard. Lou looked on as Bobby was loaded up, and the two friends looked at each other knowing that it wouldn't be too long before they would be together again.

Shelley was slightly upset at the two horses parting again but she was more determined to get them together as often as possible.

Lou settled into his new yard and soon made some new friends, he became closer to Camilla and the other horses that he would soon know so much better.

He felt more of a connection with John now and he knew that their riding was going to be a learning experience for both of them.

Tiffany and John, would often go out on a hack together and on the occasions when they passed the house with the oak tree in the paddock where Lou had his awful experiences, he did exactly what Bobby had told him to and took in every bit of information.

John had no idea of what Lou was taking in and although he was apprehensive when passing the house, he seemed to forget about it quite quickly.

'Look at the condition of the place, Lou, and try to find out if there are any horses there,' Bobby had told him.

Within a few weeks Lou had all the information he needed, there was a little pony in the shoddily built stable and only on two occasions did he see the pony in the small paddock.

Tiffany and John had seen the little pony in the paddock, but she appeared to be fairly healthy although a little underweight.

It wasn't unusual for horses to lose weight and then suddenly put it on so they weren't that suspicious, although the state of the paddock concerned them.

There was very little grass and Lou couldn't see any hay nets anywhere.

He knew that the pony was suffering with her head hung low and that the conditions in which she was kept were not good.

He had also seen the boy Billy, who by now had grown taller and bigger. Just the sight of that boy brought back some painful memories of being whipped by Billy and left without food or water for days on end. Lou figured that the little pony was probably suffering the same fate, or even worse. Lou looked around and saw the two-wheeled trap that had caused him so much pain and shuddered.

Every time they passed the house, Lou and Camilla would neigh and give the little pony some encouragement and let her know they were watching her. Lou had told Camilla about his time at that awful place and they were hoping that Tiffany and John would take some action. It wasn't unusual for horses to neigh when they saw other horses or ponies so this went a little unnoticed at first.

Eventually Tiffany and John began to notice that Lou and Camilla were neighing to the little pony more and more. They

could see that the pony was only about two-years-old, but from a distance they couldn't fully make out its condition.

'Look at that little pony,' said Tiffany. 'It doesn't look very happy does it?'

'No. It looks like it needs some fattening up too,' said John.

'We'll have to ride past here more often and keep an eye on it,' John said with some concern.

On one occasion when they passed the house, the boy had seen Lou and Camilla coming up the road so he came closer to the fence as they passed.

He knew straight away that Lou was the little horse that had escaped from him over three years ago; it was the markings on his legs and belly that were so distinguishable. Billy was really jealous of the man on his back.

'Nice horses,' he shouted. He had considered telling Tiffany and John that he had once owned Lou, but decided against it.

'Yes, they are aren't they, which is more than we can say for your pony,' John shouted back in a harsh voice.

The boy had to think quickly, he knew that he could be reported for not looking after a pony properly.

'Oh yes, I just got her and I'm getting her back to fitness as she was neglected and abandoned.'

There was something about the boy's voice that didn't sound right and they knew that given the state of the paddock and stables the boy couldn't offer the conditions that even a small pony needed.

There was a slightly awkward silence and the two trotted on, they were even more committed to keep an eye on the little pony. 'We really do need to come by more often,' said John. 'I'm not comfortable about things here and if we don't monitor things who will?'

***

'Hi, Dad,' Shelley said as John answered the phone one evening.

'How would you like to come over with Tiffany and the horses and have a ride out next weekend? I will arrange to have you both collected by my friend Deb who has a horsebox.'

'That would be great, Shelley, I'm sure Bobby and Lou will like it too.' John said excitedly.

'I know Lyn would love to see Camilla again,' Shelley added.

John asked Tiffany who was only too pleased to ride elsewhere for a change.

The following weekend Camilla and Lou were transported to Lyn's yard and were put into a field with Bobby. The three of them were soon playing games and chasing each other around the field with Shelley, Tiffany, Deb and John looking on enjoying every moment.

After an hour or so they brought the horses in for grooming and then they were tacked up and ready for a ride out.

John wasn't as experienced in tacking up a horse as Shelley and Tiffany, and so they had to wait for him.

John led Lou to the mounting block but Lou wasn't quite close enough, so John led him round again and tried to mount.

Again Lou was slightly too far out from the mounting block but John was aware that he was keeping the girls waiting and tried to mount Lou from the block.

He put his foot in the stirrup and tried to cock his leg over the saddle but being unbalanced Lou leapt forward panic-stricken.

Lou started bucking and spun round quickly dumping John in a heap on the floor.

There were a couple of girls in the yard who grabbed hold of Lou's reins.

John picked himself up from the floor and although he wasn't severely hurt, his pride was dented. He knew that the first thing he should do is calm Lou and get someone to hold him, which he knew he should have done in the first place.

Once John was safely on Lou the three of them set off. It wasn't long before the incident was behind them and they were enjoying a canter along a tree lined bridle path.

As they settled down to a gentle walk, Shelley pulled Bobby up next to Lou.

'Dad, I'm so sorry about what happened in the yard, I should have helped you to get on Lou before I got on Bobby.'

Shelley knew her dad had learnt a lot over the last few months, but she forgot that he still had much to learn despite having ridden horses on and off for many years. One thing

Shelley knew more than anyone was that continued training for both horse and rider was needed. When they had completed their ride, the horses were cooled off and put in the field for an hour while John, Shelley and Tiffany went off for some lunch.

When they were alone in the field, Lou and Camilla told Bobby about the little pony and the boy who was supposed to be looking after her.

'Don't worry about it,' Bobby said. 'We will make sure she is OK, we just need to work out a plan.'

'What can we do?' Lou replied.

'Leave it to me, I will work something out and let you know.'

Bobby wasn't quite sure what he could do at this time but it wouldn't be long before the little pony would be liberated.

The three horses managed to get down to some proper grazing and some chasing around the field, which took their mind off of their impending plans.

A few weeks later, Shelley took Bobby over to ride with Tiffany and her dad around the local area and bridle paths that Lou and Camilla had got to know so well. Bobby loved it as it took him away from his usual riding areas that he enjoyed, but riding a new path was always a welcome change.

'It is important that we ride past that little pony at some point today,' Bobby told Camilla and Lou.

'If John or Tiffany try to take us in a different direction then we must resist until they give in, it's the only way we can help the little one.'

Bobby had no need to worry about riding past the house where the little pony was stabled as Tiffany had planned to ride past regularly to keep an eye on her.

When they had tacked up the horses, John, Tiffany and Shelley set off in the direction of the little pony.

John had practised mounting Lou from the mounting block, and by now Lou was accustomed to what he needed to do to have John get into the saddle safely.

Tiffany explained her concerns for the little pony to Shelley and asked if there was anything they could do.

'Of course we can do something,' said Shelley. 'We might not be allowed to go on to the property and check things out for ourselves, but we can report the owner to the RSPCA if we suspect that the pony is being mistreated.'

When they arrived at the house the pony was nowhere to be seen, which worried them slightly.

'Where do you suppose the pony is?' Tiffany asked Shelley.

'I don't know but I'm not leaving here without finding out.'

At that point Bobby started neighing as loud as he could and Lou and Camilla followed suit.

'What's got into them?' John asked Shelley in a concerned voice.

'I don't know Dad, something has startled them.'

Bobby was rearing up and making plenty of noise as his shoes clattered to the ground.

The three horses made such a commotion between them that it attracted the attention of the people in the house who were now looking through the window.

The boy who was now about nineteen years old came out of the house to see what was going on. The sight of him made Lou very angry.

'Why are your horses making such a din?' the boy asked.

'Oh something spooked them that's all,' Shelley replied in an instant.

The horses calmed down, which gave John the opportunity to ask the boy a question.

'Where is your little pony today?' he asked in a polite tone.

'Oh she's in the stable laying down; she's got an infection in her leg and can't stand for too long.'

At that point the little pony poked its head over the door of the stable and gave out a high-pitched neigh.

Bobby knew that the noise they had made had alerted the little pony and given her the strength to get up. It was all part of his plan.

'Do you mind if I take a look at your pony?' Shelley asked the boy. 'I work with horses on a regular basis and may be able to help you.'

'Oh it's OK thanks, she'll be fine,' the boy said slightly flustered.

'It's no problem,' said Shelley as she climbed down off of Bobby.

'Here, Dad, hold Bobby for me a moment please.'

'Honestly, you don't need to do anything,' the boy said as Shelley entered the gate.

'Oh it's no problem, as I said I work with horses and I may be able to give you some good advice.'

There was no way Shelley was going to leave without assessing the state of the little pony that day.

'We've phoned the vet,' the boy said lying to her. 'He's coming out this afternoon.'

'Oh, that's great. Which vet do you use?' Shelley replied hoping to catch the boy out.

'I can't remember who it is - my mum called them.'

The boy's mum was nowhere to be seen, so Shelley assumed that the boy was alone. His mum was actually watching out of the window as she knew what kind of trouble she could be in if she was accused of not looking after a horse properly.

Shelley knew the boy was lying and was surprised that he had not stopped her by the time she reached the stable.

Shelley opened the stable door and it was immediately clear that the little pony was in need of food, water and immediate medical attention. The straw bed on the stable floor was damp and had not been cleaned for what appeared to be many days or even weeks.

There was a small bucket in the corner and Shelley could see that what little water was in it, was dirty.

There were no signs of hay nets or any other food for the pony.

The little pony looked up at Shelley with glassy eyes as if to say 'thank you'.

She had an infection in her front leg, which was an open wound that looked very painful.

Shelley knew that the treatment would be costly and by the looks of the house and the stables she feared that the boy and his family would not put the little pony's needs above anything else.

She didn't want to cause a scene with the boy in case he moved the little pony somewhere else where she couldn't track her down when the rescue team arrived.

'Would you mind getting some warm water in a bowl and a fresh towel so that I can clean her wound, and while we are here can we fill her water bucket?'

The boy willingly agreed and within minutes the wound was washed and the water bucket was filled with fresh water.

'OK, well I'm glad you have the vet coming - good luck,' Shelley said in a cheery tone.

The boy felt confident and just as the three riders were starting to walk off, he couldn't help boasting, 'Hey, that horse Jack used to be mine,' the boy exclaimed as he pointed to Lou.

'Someone stole him from me.'

Shelley couldn't believe what she was hearing; the boy was clearly ignorant of his responsibilities towards caring for horses she thought. He must have known that he could have been prosecuted for his ill treatment of Lou. However, the boy had clearly been caught up in his excitement at seeing his old horse again and didn't realise the gravity of the situation.

'Really?' Shelley said as she brought Bobby to a halt.

She turned Bobby around and told her dad and Tiffany to stay where they were.

'Oh that's interesting,' Shelley said. 'We were trying to find the owner when he was found wandering down a country lane not too far from here.'

The boy became quite excited; he thought he might be in a position to claim his horse back. He had been struck by Lou's beauty some weeks previous when he had seen John and Tiffany riding past his house.

'Well now that he's been found and you know who owned him, I'd like to have him back,' said the boy stupidly.

'Well I'm not sure about the legal situation but in theory if you can prove you owned the horse you call Jack, when he was found, then I suppose he would still be yours.'

The boy was suddenly overjoyed at the thoughts running through his mind.

Shelley was just trying to buy time and gain the boy's confidence, but she was already planning to call Suzie and stage a rescue mission.

As they parted company, Shelley was confident that the boy's lack of understanding was going to be his undoing.

After catching up with her dad and Tiffany and telling them about the conversation she had with the boy, they rode back to the stable. They sorted the horses out and immediately drove to see Suzie.

Lou had witnessed what was going on and was happy that he had a part to play in the possible rescue of the little pony.

Suzie felt very angry and wanted to call the RSPCA and go and collect the little pony straight away, but after hearing that the boy was responsible for Lou's injuries and mistreatment, she calmed down and arranged to see her lawyer the next day. The plan was to rescue the pony after speaking to the lawyer.

They had to get the boy to confess that he had owned Lou at the time he was found in that terrible condition and getting him to own up in front of an RSPCA officer was the next objective.

The following day, Shelley arranged for Bobby to be collected and taken back to Lyn's yard.

The same day Shelley, Suzie and an undercover RSPCA officer visited the boy to discuss the legal ownership of Lou; well that's what the boy was led to believe.

Suzie and the RSPCA officer had contacted the police and had arranged for a rescue vehicle to collect the little pony once they had obtained a confession from the boy that he had owned Lou or as the boy knew him at that time, Jack.

'Hi,' Shelley said as the boy answered the front door.

'This is Peter and Jane who now own 'Jack' and they want to discuss the ownership of him with you. This wasn't exactly how things should be conducted by law, but it was the only way in which they felt they could extract the truth. After all the boy and his family had no respect for the law.

'Come in,' the boy said excitedly. 'My mum is in and she can confirm that Jack was mine.'

'Mum can you come in here for a minute?' The boy's mum entered the room and once the reason for the people being there was explained to her, she immediately confirmed that Jack was once their horse. Although there was no official paperwork, verbal confessions witnessed by officials were acceptable in court.

The boy was so excited that he didn't even question why owners of such a lovely horse would want to give it back to a previous owner who had made no attempt to claim the horse back. The RSPCA officer, Shelley and Suzie, witnessed the confession and all they needed to do now was rescue the little pony.

'Can we see your little pony?' Shelley said in a friendly voice.

'Of course, the vet saw her yesterday and put her on some medication.' The boy was lying and knew he couldn't refuse to let them see the pony for fear of them becoming suspicious.

As soon as Suzie knew the little pony was there she walked off and made a quick call to the rescue team who were waiting around the corner with a horsebox.

A local police officer also accompanied the rescue party in case the boy or his family members resisted the rescue of the pony.

When the RSPCA officer saw the little pony he immediately pulled his identification card out and explained that due to the poor state of the pony, it would need to be removed immediately from the stable. He also explained that due to the boy owning up to being responsible for Lou's plight over three years before, they were not prepared to give the boy another chance.

'Mum! Mum! They want to take Star,' the boy shouted through the back door of the house.

The boy's mum ran out of the house and approached the RSPCA officer shouting and threatening him.

'I have to warn you, madam, that the police will be here shortly and if this pony doesn't receive treatment very soon it will die.'

At that moment, the rescue party arrived with the police

officer and straight away the boy's mum knew that she would not be able to talk her way out of the situation.

The little pony was loaded into the horsebox and a police officer took down the details of both the boy and his mother.

They were warned that they may be prosecuted under the Protection of Animals Act and that they would be contacted once the investigations were concluded.

The police officer made arrangements to come back and speak to them once he had spoken to the RSPCA officer and had obtained a veterinary report.

The police officer left the property while the mother and the boy went back into the house arguing about why he had let people into the house and onto the property without telling her.

In truth she had been just as excited about getting Lou back as the boy was.

VIII

ROSIE

As soon as the little pony was unloaded and put into a temporary stable at the sanctuary, Suzie took photographs of her wounds to support any future prosecution, as was usual.

The little pony was in a very poor state and although she didn't look quite as bad as Lou had when he arrived at the sanctuary, she had yet to be inspected by a vet.

The pony was given some food and water and the open wound on her leg was dressed as soon as she arrived at the sanctuary. A rug was put over her and her stable was prepared with a newly laid thick bed of wood chips; it was clear that she wouldn't be able to stand for too long, so making her comfortable was important.

Just as Lou was monitored throughout the night, so was Star.

Suzie arrived in the morning to take over from the two people she had left to monitor the new arrival through the night, but Star had difficulty getting to her feet.

Suzie had phoned the vet the previous day and was expecting her to arrive sometime within the next couple of hours.

Suzie had seen many horses and ponies with a range of illnesses and diseases, but she knew that Star was really suffering. She hoped that they had rescued her in time and was really concerned that the little one wouldn't make it.

When the vet arrived Suzie led her directly to Star, who Suzie had affectionately re-named Rosie.

After a thorough examination the vet suspected that Rosie was suffering from disease of the lungs, causing heavy congestion in the nose and mouth, which made it difficult for her to breathe normally.

Rosie was given some medicine for the infection in her leg and she was much more comfortable

Although Rosie was suffering, she felt more comfortable than she had for a long time and she also knew that the people around her were kind and that she was being cared for.

The farrier arrived to fit shoes to some of the other horses and ponies and trim Rosie's sore hooves. But as Rosie was too traumatised by her experience at the hands of the boy and the squalid conditions that she had been kept in, it was decided that it would have to wait. It would be a couple of days before the true condition of Rosie was known.

The laboratory tests confirmed that Rosie was indeed suffering from a lung disease.

Rosie was monitored during the next few days and nights, but her condition deteriorated, despite the medication and efforts of the sanctuary staff.

On the fifth day that Rosie was at the sanctuary Suzie called the vet to have Rosie checked over again to see if anything could be done to help her condition.

The vet arrived and after giving Rosie a full check-up it was decided that she was very ill and suffering too much.

'I'm sorry Suzie, I'm afraid that the kindest thing to do for Rosie is to have her put down, the disease will take her if not.'

As Suzie looked down at the little pony lying there looking up at her, she could feel her eyes filling up with tears.

Suzie and her staff had seen ponies and horses come into the sanctuary that were too ill to save, but it never got any easier to witness the suffering.

Rosie was collected the next day and taken to a place to be put to sleep, which depressed the mood of the sanctuary workers for many days and weeks. The only thing that helped was that there were many other horses and ponies that had been rescued and were going from strength to strength.

The difficult nature of animal welfare was the whole focus of the horse and pony sanctuary but they had helpful links with many other charities and it was this pulling together that drove these special people on to continue their work in very upsetting times. Whether it was dogs, cats, horses or any other suffering animals, the volunteers regularly got together as a collective group to support each other and share their experiences.

People who could openly let horses and ponies become ill or malnourished always angered Suzie. Unfortunately in many cases it was impossible to track down those who were responsible.

Things were different with Rosie and as a result of finding her, they had found out who was responsible for Lou's suffering.

Suzie spoke to her legal advisor about how the family had let down both Rosie and Lou and it was agreed that they would put a case together to have the family prosecuted.

Suzie knew it was going to take months or even years to get it to court but she was determined to succeed. Suzie had many court cases pending and this was one of the fundamental reasons for her determination to see justice done. She had been through the process many times before and knew the procedures required for a successful case. She gradually built her file with witness statements and supporting evidence such as photographs and vets statements. The plan was to bring the case for the death of Rosie and the ill treatment of Lou at the same time. It took several months for all of the paperwork to be put in place and another eight months before official paperwork was served on the family with a court date.

Shelley and John were told about the sad loss of Rosie, which made them both cry.

John and Tiffany felt particularly sad and felt slightly guilty as they had seen the little pony about two months earlier.

'If only we had reported it then,' Tiffany said to John in a sad tone, 'perhaps she would still be alive.'

'It's not our fault, Tiffany, the boy told us that the little pony had been neglected and that he was getting her back to health.'

John remembered that the boy seemed nervous, but they could hardly accuse him of being cruel without evidence, which is why he and Tiffany took the decision to keep an eye on the pony.

'We did all we could and we weren't to know that she was suffering that much.'

As much as John tried to pacify himself and Tiffany, it played on his mind and he could not stop thinking about poor Rosie. In the first few weeks after Rosie had gone, John would often find that as soon as he thought about her his eyes would well up and the tears would roll down his cheeks.

He had so much respect for Suzie and her staff but he knew it was a job that he could never do himself.

John and Tiffany stopped riding past the house and as far as Lou and Camilla were concerned the little pony was safe and being cared for at the sanctuary.

Two weeks after Rosie had died; a Welsh Cob called Harvey arrived at Lyn's yard to be broken in by Shelley.

Harvey had been at the sanctuary for about four months and although he wasn't in a terrible condition when he arrived, he was very underweight.

He had been found in a field and had been tethered to a rope attached to a stake that only allowed him a few metres of slack. The grass all around him had been eaten away and the ground was completely worn where he had been walking around in circles. It was clear that he had been abandoned but his hooves and general health was above average for the type of rescue horses that Suzie usually took in to the sanctuary.

It wasn't long before Bobby and Harvey met and discovered that they both had links with the sanctuary.

'So what's been happening down at the sanctuary lately?' Bobby asked Harvey when they were grazing in the field one sunny autumn afternoon.

Harvey had no idea that it was as a result of Bobby's plan that Rosie had been rescued and he started to tell him about the little pony and what had led to her death.

'What do you mean she died?' Bobby said bringing his head up swiftly and looking at Harvey with his ears pricked up.

'She was rescued wasn't she?'

'Well she was rescued but she was so ill she couldn't be saved.'

Harvey was curious at Bobby's surprised response.

Bobby explained to Harvey about how Lou and Camilla had found out about the little pony being held in those squalid conditions and the plan that they had hatched to have her rescued.

'Oh I'm so sorry, Bobby, you must be devastated.'

'I am, Harvey, and I don't know if Lou and Camilla know what has happened.'

Harvey could see the tears in Bobby's eyes as he turned away, he knew he needed to be alone and pretended that he hadn't seen the tears.

'I need to get a message to Lou and Camilla somehow to let them know what's happened,' Bobby said once he had composed himself.

Bobby decided that the only chance that he had to tell Lou and Camilla about little Rosie was to get Shelley to take him there.

He decided to behave in a way that Shelley would know that he was pining for something and it only took a couple of days before Shelley recognised that something was wrong.

'I think I'm going to take Bobby over to see Lou,' she told Lyn one morning. 'I'm sure he's missing him'.

So it was arranged that the following weekend Bobby would be transported over to Lou's stables for a weekend of riding with Lou and Camilla.

The day came and Bobby was loaded into the horsebox for the short trip.

'Hey! Look,' Lou said to Camilla as they were playing in a field one afternoon 'that looks like the horsebox that Bobby comes over in.'

The two horses raced across the field so that they could see if the horsebox pulled into the yard.

To their complete surprise it pulled into the yard and stopped.

'Do you suppose its Bobby or another horse?' Camilla said as she looked at Lou inquisitively.

'Well I haven't heard John or Tiffany talking about Bobby coming over, so I'm not sure.'

Lou and Camilla looked on with excitement as they recognised both Shelley and Claire getting out of the car.

They couldn't quite see the horse, which was slightly obscured by a screen, but as soon as they saw the shiny chestnut coat they knew it could only be Bobby.

They made such a loud noise with their neighs and jumping up and down on their front legs that all the other horses wondered what was going on.

Bobby could hear Lou and Camilla and knew straight away that they were watching on from some vantage point. He neighed back as loud as he could to let them know he had heard them.

Shelley and Claire had witnessed the scene and knew that bringing Bobby over to spend some time with Lou was a good idea.

Once Bobby was unloaded he was immediately taken to the field to be with Lou and Camilla.

Shelley and Claire stood watching them and they could see how happy they were at seeing one another other again, although Bobby wasn't rushing about as usual, which they couldn't understand it.

Bobby knew that Lou and Camilla were going to be very upset with the news that he was going to deliver to them and led them to the other side of the field, slowly.

'Hey Bobby that's not like you, you normally want to race us across the field to show us how fast you are.'

Bobby walked on slowly and glanced at them both with a sad look on his face.

'What is it, Bobby?' asked Camilla, slightly concerned by now.

Shelley and Claire went back to the horsebox and unloaded the tack.

'What a great surprise, Bobby, we didn't know you were coming over,' Lou said excitedly, but he was aware that something was not quite right.

'We have some great news to tell you, Bobby,' said Camilla with pride. She was just about to tell him about how the little pony had been rescued.

Camilla really wanted to cement her friendship with Bobby by giving him some terrific news and was surprised at his unusually sad demeanour.

'What's the matter Bobby?' said Lou. 'You don't look happy to be here.'

'I've got some bad news for you I'm afraid,' said Bobby with a sad look on his face.

'Rosie didn't make it; she was too ill to save and had to be put to sleep.'

Lou and Camilla looked at each other in shock.

One moment they were feeling really happy and within seconds that happiness disappeared and was replaced with a gut wrenching feeling of dread and sickness.

Lou couldn't even bring himself to ask Bobby for the details and slowly turned and walked away.

As Lou walked off across the field Bobby explained to Camilla what had happened. Camilla took it all in and told Bobby that she would go and talk to Lou.

Of course it was very upsetting for Camilla, but it was worse for Lou as he had suffered in the same place at the hands of the same people who were responsible for Rosie's death.

As Camilla followed Lou, her eyes filled with tears as she remembered the little pony she saw in the shoddily built stable. What more could we have done she questioned herself.

'Come on, Lou, we did all we could,' she told him as she walked to his side.

Lou's head was hung lower than she had ever seen it before and rather than make him feel awkward and talk about Rosie, she just stood by him in silence.

Bobby knew to leave Camilla and Lou alone while they took in the sad news. He knew that Lou would not want anyone to see him crying.

Lou eventually came out of his reverie and lifted his head.

'We should go and be with Bobby,' he said to Camilla.

'He's come to give us the news, but I'm sure he is as upset as we are.'

After they walked back to Bobby, Lou knew that he had to be strong and find out what had happened.

Bobby explained things in as much detail as he dare, he told them that the boy and his family were going to be prosecuted.

'What does that mean, Bobby?' said Lou. 'Does that mean they will be whipped?'

'I don't think so, Lou, but I'm sure they won't be able to keep horses any more and more than likely they will be put in a human stable and not let out for a long time.'

For the rest of the day, the three horses just grazed in the field and hardly spoke.

It was a sombre atmosphere and all they could do was think about Rosie.

The weekend turned out to be very sunny and they had some good rides out, which helped them to deal with the sad news.

Bobby was taken back to his yard after the weekend and although it was difficult telling Lou and Camilla about Rosie, he also knew that the longer he left it, the more difficult it would be, he was glad that it had been him that had told them the sad news.

IX

SAMSON

Lou was going from strength to strength and had become very confident with John as his sole rider. He loved being brought in from the fields by John, who would spoil him with carrots and fresh apples before having his main evening dinner.

Apart from hacking out with Tiffany and Camilla regularly, John had entered Lou into a show in hand competition, where Lou would be brushed and groomed with all his tack oiled and looking like new. John would wear his best jodhpurs and riding boots with a new white shirt and tie and black riding jacket. Although it was show in hand, where the rider walks by the horse and has to stop at various points and trot by the horse's side, all the proper riding gear had to be worn.

John and Lou had won quite a few rosettes and were starting to become well known in the local equine circles.

Lou was a handsome looking horse and, with his typical Hackney trot, he was a delight to watch.

He had never really known what he wanted to be and he can always remember when Bobby was rolling around on the ground when he had asked him what a show jumper was.

Lou knew he couldn't jump fences because of the operation that he had when he was young, but Camilla had told him that he would possibly make a good dressage horse.

'What's dressage, Camilla?' he asked innocently, he knew that Camilla wouldn't laugh at him like Bobby did, but he still felt a bit embarrassed that he didn't know.

Lou had heard that horses were bred for dressage but he didn't really know what it involved.

'Dressage takes years of training and hours of practice,' she told him.

'Horse and rider must move as one, with hardly any movement, but just slight pressure with the rider's knees or reins as communication,' she went on to explain it as like ballet on horseback.

'There's no quick way to learn dressage Lou, either for the rider or the horse.'

Lou was struck by her explanation and since he knew that John wouldn't risk jumping him he hoped that he would learn some dressage.

Lou was especially excited when he found out that dressage is sometimes performed to music.

That was it; he could now tell Bobby what he wanted to be.

'I can't wait to see Bobby,' he told Camilla. Lou explained to her about how Bobby had rolled around on the ground when he had asked what a show jumper was.

Camilla smiled and felt sorry for Lou, although she understood why Bobby found it funny.

'Don't worry Lou. I'm sure you will be good at dressage if you get the chance to learn it.'

Lou had seen Oscar, his field mate, and Oscar's owner, Jayne, in the schooling area doing some strange trotting and other things that Lou found a bit odd. And he was sure that this is what was called dressage.

It was late autumn now and Lou and John were attending the last of the show in hand competitions for the year. They had done really well and John knew that Lou had so much more potential.

Shelley had mentioned to her dad that Lou would make a good dressage horse one day, and although he wasn't a natural, he was very handsome and had lovely movement.

John thought about this and read up on dressage training. He decided that he was ready for the long road ahead. The next day, he booked a dressage lesson on Lou with Julian who was an international horse-jumping professional who had horses at the stables.

Julian had a wealth of experience in all disciplines and was a very charismatic person. John had been told that Julian knew how to train horses and riders and John could see that he had a connection with horses that was unmatched.

John and Lou started their dressage lessons with Julian. John was surprised that the lessons started with many weeks of basic training. He had to concentrate on getting the smallest things perfect.

Lou found it quite strange, as he was used to more energetic work. These new precise and careful exercises took a lot of concentration from them both.

It was two weeks before Christmas and Suzie had been in touch with John to tell him that the court date was due in two weeks.

John, Shelley and Tiffany were required to attend the court proceedings as witnesses, and they were only too happy to do so.

The day of the court hearing came and it was expected to be a successful outcome for the prosecution.

Everybody filed into the courtroom and the solicitors sat at the front of the court awaiting the arrival of the family who were accused of cruelty to animals.

Their solicitor had seen them the day before and had warned them that the case against them was very strong, and that at worst they could expect a custodial sentence.

He also told them that at best they would be given a big fine and banned from owning animals for many years.

As the throng of people sat in the courtroom and the public gallery filled up, the accused were nowhere to be seen.

The judge arrived and duly read out the charges knowing that the accused family were not in attendance. After giving the solicitor a stern warning that his clients had wasted court time and that he would be issuing a summons for the family to report to the police station, he dismissed the witnesses and court staff.

Suzie was fuming; she had worked so hard to bring the case and had spent more than she had hoped on legal costs. She knew it would be worth it in the end, but it always frustrated her when animal abusers showed so much contempt for the law. The family could not avoid their moment in court forever as a warrant was put out for their arrest and the court hearing would be rescheduled to another date.

The police were assigned to deliver the summons to the family and when they arrived at the property it was clear that the family had left.

There were no vehicles on the property, and the two-wheeled trap and other trailers that were normally there, were gone.

Upon their investigation it was found that the family had been renting the property and had not left a forwarding address.

The police had no leads to where they had gone and other priorities took over.

Suzie tried to keep the pressure on to track the family down but she too had to concentrate on running the sanctuary.

The court issued various summonses but could only post them to the address that they had on record, so they never actually reached the family.

As the winter months passed by and spring approached, John and Lou were making good but slow progress with the dressage lessons. John found it very difficult and Lou was also starting to doubt himself.

Shelley and John would often arrange for rides out on Bobby, Lou and Camilla.

The three horses would swap stories of what they were doing and what they hoped to do.

They never really spoke about Rosie but they never forgot about her either. All of them knew that if they started to talk about her, that their mood would be such that they would not enjoy their time together. They were still grieving and there would be plenty of time to come to terms with her loss.

Shelley had been giving Bobby jumping lessons and was astounded at his ability.

'I'm jumping three feet now,' Bobby told Lou and Camilla with his chest pumped out and his head held high.

Although Lou and Camilla were the best of friends, Bobby had made an impact on Camilla from the first time they met.

She started to develop a soft spot for him and every so often when they were in the field grazing, she would try to spend a little time alone with him where they would groom each other and rub their necks together.

Bobby was an extremely handsome horse and loved the attention especially from Camilla as she was a very beautiful mare.

As spring turned into summer Shelley and her dad would alternate when Bobby would be taken to see Lou for the weekend and vice versa, making sure they had plenty of time together. Camilla would always join in with the reunions and the three horses formed a strong bond.

Camilla was very fit, she could easily keep up with Bobby and Lou in a gallop and the three of them enjoyed racing each other.

There was never any animosity between them, and they knew that the riders were in control of things as much as they were.

Their rides out started to become longer and on the odd occasion they would be loaded into a large horsebox and taken to different place to ride just for a change of scenery.

It was on one of these rides away from their local riding areas that Lou noticed something that startled him. They had been cantering down a wide tree-lined bridle path, which led onto a narrow country lane that they had to cross to get to the next bridle path.

Out of the corner of his eye and over the small hedgerow he noticed a small opening, which led to a run-down cottage. In the front garden was the two wheeled trap that he had grown up to hate.

He stopped and reared up a little to get Bobby and Camilla's attention, neighing as he did so.

'Whoa, Lou what's up boy,' said John slightly startled at the suddenness of Lou's reaction.

Instinctively John looked around to see what had startled Lou and with his advantage of being able to see clearly over the hedge, he knew exactly what had startled Lou.

He calmed Lou and called to Shelley and Tiffany.

'Look over there,' he said. 'That's the trap that belongs to the boy that caused Rosie's death'.

'Do you suppose the family are living here now?' Shelley asked.

John had to think quickly.

'I don't know, but let's move on as we don't want them to see us if they are here.'

As they walked on they looked over the hedge but there were no signs of life. John decided that he wanted to establish whether the family were living in the cottage before taking any further action.

'I will come back on foot and check the place out later,' said John.

They made their way back to the stables via a different route so as not to be discovered by the family, if in fact they did live at the cottage.

Later that day, just as dusk was approaching, John decided that he should try to find out who lived in the cottage and drove to the country lane. He parked up some way from the cottage in a small lay-by and made the rest of the way on foot.

He took a pair of binoculars with him and wore dark clothing in order to provide some camouflage

As he walked up the bridle path he could see the cottage through some small gaps in the hedge. The hedge was about six feet high and thick enough for him to hide behind.

He looked up and down the bridle path just to make sure there were no dog walkers or ramblers coming and pushed himself into the hedge to get a better view of the cottage.

The lights were on in the cottage and it wasn't long before he saw movement inside.

With the binoculars pressed up against his eyes, he couldn't quite make out the people inside and decided to venture closer.

He climbed over the barbed wire fence and hid behind an old water tank until it was dark. As dusk turned to night,

John waited and within half an hour of hiding behind the water tank he had seen the boy, his mother and a man who he had not seen before.

'Well, well, well,' he said to himself. 'They thought they had got away with the court case.'

He couldn't wait to get back and tell Shelley and Tiffany the good news.

Once he had told them the news, Shelley immediately telephoned Suzie.

'You're not going to believe this Suzie, but we know where the family who mistreated Rosie are living.'

'What did you say?' asked Suzie hardly able to believe the news.

Shelley explained the events of the day and it was left to Suzie to plan the next steps.

It wasn't long before an arrest warrant was prepared, and just two days later the family were arrested. The boy, his mother and her boyfriend were taken into custody.

Because they had never received the several summonses that had been sent to them and would probably have ignored them in any case, it was decided to keep them locked up for the three months that it would take to bring the case to court.

'You can't lock us up,' the family protested. 'It was only a horse after all.'

'Who is going to look after our dogs and cats?'

'The RSPCA have put them into rescue homes,' the policeman explained.

'We have rights you know.'

'Horses have rights too,' they were often told by the prison guards.

'We could always treat you the same way as you treated those poor horses,' one of the guards reminded them.

What surprised Suzie and the RSPCA more than anything was that behind the cottage in a tiny paddock was a little one-year-old pony.

Thankfully it looked as though they had only just got him and although he was underweight, he was in reasonably good health.

The pony was taken to the sanctuary and as usual Suzie chose a new name for him, he would be known as Samson.

He was a black Irish Cob and had a lovely nature. It seemed clear to the sanctuary workers that from day one Samson knew he had been rescued from a very hard and lonely existence. He was cooperative and absolutely adorable. He hadn't really liked the name of Blacky that his previous owners had given him but his new name made him feel special. It was a good start for the fortunate little pony.

Whilst the new case was being prepared and a new court date set, Bobby resumed his show jumping training and Lou and John continued with their lessons with Julian.

Camilla was happy to just hack out with them whenever she could and enjoyed her continued schooling with Tiffany. Camilla had no real plans to be anything other than a rider's horse as she really enjoyed some simple jumping and long rides out in woods and fields.

***

The court date arrived and all of the people involved in the case were there for the hearing.

Proceedings took just over two hours and such was the evidence against Billy and his mother they were each fined £20,000 and given the maximum amount of time in prison of six months for cruelty to animals. They were also banned from keeping any animals for life, and that included looking after other people's animals.

The man who was living at the house was freed as it couldn't be fully established if he was involved in any wrong doing.

As far as Suzie and the others were concerned, they should have been locked up for years. She was always petitioning for prison sentences to be longer and could never understand why they weren't.

It was however a satisfactory outcome and Suzie treated everyone to a meal out to celebrate their efforts.

***

The next couple of years passed by in much the same way, with Lou and Camilla hacking out together regularly and Bobby being brought over from time to time.

John had been working hard with Lou on some technical riding skills and they were doing OK. This was due partly to Lou's field mate, Oscar, who had won dressage competitions and had lots of helpful advice for Lou.

John and Lou had a great life but Lou was so much more at home hacking out and enjoying the open fields, rather than with the strict confines of dressage.

They put the time in but after a few months, John knew that although he and Lou had tried their hardest to be good at dressage, they weren't going to get to the top so John decided to concentrate on just enjoying what Lou wanted.

John decided that to give Lou the best training for good technical riding he would need to have plenty of additional training with Julian, a professional trainer, and forget about the dressage lessons.

'Flat work and posture is important if you want to get the best from Lou,' Julian would say.

Julian had been there, done it and got the tee shirt, from National to International show jumping events to breeding and showing some of the finest horses in the land.

When Julian wasn't around there were others who were more than prepared to help John progress and Mark was one of them. He had been at the top of his game and had worked with many of the top show jumpers over the years preparing their horses for national events. Quite often John would call on Mark to assist him if Lou was being troublesome, as he could be from time to time. Mark also gave John flatwork lessons on Lou to keep them both in good shape.

The yard was a great place to be and although John would have liked to spend more time with Lou, his work commitments often got in the way. Shelley continued to help her dad with his riding skills, after all he wasn't a natural rider and had to work hard at keeping his riding skills up to scratch.

Over the course of time John and Lou became good friends with all the horse owners and horses in the yard and many good rides out were had.

There were a wide range of horses at the stables and Lou knew them all.

Each horse had its own personality and whether they met in the fields, the school or had the opportunity to hack out together, all of the horses had the greatest respect for Lou. Lou had worked out the various horses' characters and treated them accordingly. He had made up nicknames for them all. There was Shy Phoebe, Dessie the Show Off, Little Miss Marble, Bouncing Bambi, BB the Dreamer, Roo the Protector, Lovely Bally, Oscar the Dressage King, Tommy the Tank, Glamorous Whisper, Pretty Pudding, Leggy Lexi, Zara Zoo, Perfect Puk, Hurry up Harry, Dizzy David, Gentle Gabe, Zany Zephy and a few others besides.

This was a great yard to be at in the beautiful hills of Kent.

Even though he was happy, Lou was nervous about telling Bobby that he had stopped his dressage lessons when he was next over.

'Don't worry Lou,' said Bobby. 'You tried your best and that's all you can do.'

Lou felt better after talking to his best friend and they continued to catch up on what they had been doing.

They would often talk about the competitions that Bobby had lost or won, and by now Bobby was doing really well and would often come in the top three.

Around the same time, the little pony, Samson, that had been found when the boy and his family were arrested, was due to leave the sanctuary and was moved to Lyn's yard for training.

He was three years old now, and stood at eleven hands. He had put on a fair bit of weight by now and Shelley knew that she would have to take things slowly.

She had trained a few Irish Cobs over the years and had found them to be fairly easy to break in, so she had no real worries that Samson would be any different.

After the two week isolation period that Lyn insisted on, Samson was now ready to be taken into the indoor school.

Shelley and Lyn had prepared the equipment that they would need to start to longe Sammy, as they had started to call him, and assumed that it was going to be an easy task.

'Come on Sammy, let's have you,' said Shelley as she tried to put the cavesson on.

Whereas Lou had accepted the cavesson easily, Samson was having none of it.

Although he was used to a head collar there was something about the cavesson that he didn't like.

Despite their efforts, and Shelley being as gentle as possible with him he would not let her get the cavesson over his head.

'I've never known anything like it Lyn, what do you suppose it is?'

Lyn had no idea and since he wasn't going to accept the cavesson, it was highly unlikely that he would accept a bridle and bit.

'Let's put the head collar back on him and let him get used to the school and longe lead,' Lyn suggested.

Samson allowed the head collar to be put back on and the longe lead was connected.

'OK, walk on, Sammy,' Shelley said in a gentle voice.

Samson stood as still as a rock and snorted.

'Come on Sammy, walk on,' she said in a louder voice.

She hadn't used the longing whip at this point as she wanted to get him walking before the whip was held in position.

She never whipped the horses, she just cracked the whip in the air as the sound would normally be enough to get them moving.

Shelley backed off, let out some of the longe lead and held the whip toward Samson's hind quarter.

'Walk on, Sammy, there's a good lad,' Shelley said in an even louder but friendly tone while cracking the whip.

Samson turned away from Shelley and such was his strength he dragged her across the school as she hung onto the longe lead.

Samson eventually stopped; he stood there and wasn't prepared to do anything that Shelley wanted him to do.

Despite all of the years of experience that Shelley and Lyn had, they could not get Samson to co-operate.

He would allow them to walk him around the school with a head collar and lead, but that was it.

Eventually when they had had enough of trying; Lyn and Shelley gave up. This was the first of many sessions that she had planned and she knew that it was pointless to continue right now. Never by any other tried and tested methods had they forced a horse to do what it didn't want to do.

'Perhaps he's not quite settled yet,' Lyn suggested. 'We'll give it another go tomorrow.'

They put Samson in a field with some of the other ponies and watched him as he ran off to join them.

After he had introduced himself to Harvey, who was still at Lyn's yard, and Crystal, a Palomino, who was one of Lyn's riding school horses, he started to tell them about what had just happened.

'Hmmm, Sammy they called me,' he told them angrily. 'My name is Samson and until they call me by my proper name I'm not going to do what they ask.'

Harvey and Crystal couldn't help but laugh.

'Don't worry about it, Samson, we all have our names shortened at some point.'

'But why?' Samson replied curiously.

'Oh I don't know, I think it's easier for them, they call me Harv most of the time.'

'What do they call you, Crystal?' asked Samson.

'Well actually I have always been called Crystal; I can't remember ever being called anything else.'

Samson was confused.

Harvey immediately knew that Samson was not going to give in to being called anything but his full name.

'I like Samson though,' said Samson with pride. 'It makes me sound big and strong. My name was Blacky before I was rescued so what would they have called me if I still had that name?'

'Sammy isn't such a bad name,' Harvey told him.

'But that's not my name,' replied Samson.

Harvey gave up; he knew there would be no way of changing Samson's mind.

The following day when Shelley collected Samson from his stable, she thought that rather than put the head collar on him to lead him to the school, she would put the cavesson on.

'That's it Samson,' she said as she put the cavesson on him.'

'Aha,' thought Samson, she has worked it out.

He co-operated and walked to the school with Shelley and Lyn feeling much better.

Once they were in the school Shelley attached the longe lead and with the whip in one hand and the lead in the other she started.

'OK, Sammy, walk on.'

Samson was livid and stood his ground.

'Sammy,' Shelley shouted, 'come on.'

Still Samson stood there.

'Samson, walk on,' she said in a frustrated voice.

Samson walked on.

Thank god for that Shelley thought.

Samson walked on and after two circulations Shelley tried again.

'OK, Sammy, trotting on now,' she tried as she cracked the whip slightly.

Samson stood still again.

'I don't believe this' Shelley said as she looked across at Lyn.

'Let me have a go,' Lyn said 'perhaps he's nervous.'

Shelley and Lyn swapped places.

'OK, Samson let's have you now, walking on,' Lyn said calmly.

Samson did just as he was told and things started to get better.

'Trotting on now, Samson,' Lyn said, and no sooner as she had said that Samson was trotting around the school in a good style.

Shelley couldn't make it out; she had never had problems with the basics when it came to schooling horses. 'Thank God for that,' Shelley thought.

As Lyn became more confident that she had the better of Samson, she tried to get him back to a walk.

'OK, Sammy, walking now' she said in a low and long tone of voice.

Samson stopped dead in his tracks.

'I don't believe it,' Lyn said, looking and feeling as frustrated as Shelley was just a few minutes earlier.

'I think we are going to have our work cut out with this boy,' she said.

They decided enough was enough for this session and after cooling Samson down they put him back in his stable.

'What do you think is wrong?' Shelley asked Lyn somewhat bemused.

These Irish cobs can be a bit stubborn at times, but they normally co-operate very quickly.'

'I don't know,' replied Lyn 'but we must always remember that we don't know what they have been through in life.'

'True,' Shelley said in reply 'perhaps we just need to be patient with him.'

Out in the field the next day, Samson told Harvey and Crystal what had happened and was hoping for some sort of support, but instead he received what could be more easily described as a telling off from both of them.

'Do you want to end up back at the sanctuary?' Harvey grumbled.

'Shelley and Lyn don't deserve to have awkward ponies' Crystal said in a more sympathetic tone.

'They work very hard to train all of the rescued horses and ponies so that they can go on to have good lives, so you had better take that in,' Harvey growled as he walked away.

'Just accept what you are being called and behave, please,' said Crystal as she looked at Samson how a mother would look at her own child while giving words of wisdom.

'Well if you say so,' said Samson reluctantly.

He knew he had been told off by older and wiser horses, but tried to maintain his dignity.

The following day when Shelley and Lyn collected him for his training, they thought they were going to have a hard time.

The cavesson was put on Samson and he was led into the school.

'OK, Sammy, walking on now,' Shelley said in a quiet and long tone of voice.

Samson did as he was told, although he did give her a rather cold look.

'That's better,' she said.

After Samson had walked clockwise and then anti-clockwise for about five minutes, Shelley decided to try and speed things up.

'T-t-t-t-t-rotting on now Samson' she said in a slightly faster voice.

She was amazed at how well he was responding.

The whole session went without a hitch, both Shelley and Lyn could not understand what they had done differently from the previous day.

'OK, Harvey, explain this to me,' Samson said when they were in the field grazing later that day.

'When I am in the school with Shelley, sometimes she calls me Sammy and sometimes she calls me Samson.'

'Oh' said Harvey looking up for a moment 'that's because she runs out of breath sometimes.'

Harvey hoped that his reasoning would satisfy Samson as he put his head back down to graze.

'Oh is that all,' said Samson, 'Perhaps she needs some schooling then.'

Samson was glad to have Harvey there to advise him and wandered off to graze on some fresh grass on the other side of the field.

'I think we are going to have to keep an eye on young Samson,' Harvey said to Crystal.

'I think he could end up in trouble unless he does as he is told.'

'You're right, Harvey, don't worry I will have a discreet word without seeming to be too hard on him.'

It was now late autumn and Samson had been trained over a period of eight weeks with exceptional results.

Shelley and Lyn were astounded at his willingness to learn and knew that he would be easy to place with a fosterer.

Samson had made friends with all of the horses and ponies at the yard and even Bobby had taken a shine to him. He was funny and had a mischievous but lovable character.

Bobby was reminded of himself and Lou when they were younger and playing games in the fields. Bobby could see his younger self in Samson, and found it difficult to get angry with him.

Just as Bobby used to do, Samson would often creep up behind other horses and ponies that were grazing in the field and pull their tails before running off, or chase them around and bite them gently on the withers.

On the occasions when he was too rough or became annoying, he would be put in his place by some of the higher ranking horses.

'If you carry on misbehaving or annoying other horses, then you'll be put in a field on your own,' Bobby would tell him. Although it wasn't really true, Bobby wanted Samson to calm down before the others got seriously annoyed by him and fought back.

It wasn't long before Suzie had found a suitable fosterer for Samson and the day before he was due to leave, he said his goodbyes to his friends.

It was quite a sad day for the other horses and ponies as they knew that Samson could be overly boisterous, but he was so lovable, he would be really missed.

A young girl called Emily had met the criteria to foster Samson and he was going to the same stables as Lou and Camilla. The sanctuary made their regular visits to check the facilities out, and Samson arrived at his new stables just before Christmas.

Samson was a confident young horse and before too long he knew all of the other horses and ponies quite well. He soon got up to his old tricks of teasing the others and generally having fun.

Just as Bobby had taken a liking to Samson, so did Lou when they met in the field for the first time.

'My name's Lou, what's yours?' Lou had said as he approached the new arrival.

'Oh hi, Lou, my name is Samson, nice to meet you.'

It wasn't long before the two of them were swapping stories and Lou was surprised to hear that the same boy who had mistreated him had owned Samson.

'It sounds like you had a lucky escape there, Samson, I wasn't so lucky but thankfully I escaped and was rescued.'

'When I was at the other yard,' he told Lou one day when they were in the field together, 'there was one horse there that used to tell me off sometimes.' Lou had already worked out that Samson had the potential to be trying, but he could also see that he had a certain charm.

'His name was Bobby,' said Samson. 'He was a grumpy old horse and no fun at all.'

Lou looked at Samson.

'Bobby eh, and what does Bobby look like?'

'Oh he's a Chestnut and about sixteen hands.'

Lou thought for a moment, surely he couldn't be talking about his best friend.

'And how old is this Bobby?' he asked.

'Oh I suppose he's about eight or nine years old,' Samson replied.

'And is he good at jumping?' asked Lou.

'Yes he is actually, how did you know?'

Lou was now fuming inside, he felt very protective and had to defend Bobby's honour. He wanted to shout at the little black Cob standing in front of him as he knew it was his Bobby that Samson was talking about but he had to make sure before confronting Samson about calling him a grumpy old horse.

'Who owns Bobby?' he asked Samson almost knowing what the answer would be.

'There's a horse trainer, the one that trained me actually, but she runs out of breath and calls me by different names.'

Lou was confused at what Samson had said but he still had to get him to say her name.'

'And the name of the trainer is?' he frustratingly said.

'Oh I think her name is Shelley, no respect at all,' Samson replied casually.'

'Respect... Respect... who do you think you are coming here saying Bobby is old and Grumpy'. Lou was yelling at Samson now, which caught the ear of the other horses and ponies in his and the surrounding fields.

'And as for Shelley, you said she trained you,' Lou was so angry that Samson was afraid to say anything or even move.

'Did she hurt you, or did she teach you how to be a real horse?'

'Well I suppose she taught me well, but she called me Sammy when my name is Samson.'

'Well my name is Louis-Springer and I get called Lou, Louis, boy, lad and other names, do you hear me moaning?' Lou had calmed down slightly now but the horses in the same field could still hear that he had a rather bad tempered voice.

'And tell me something else, Sammy' said Lou, making sure to use his shortened name.

'What did Bobby do to make you think he was grumpy?'

'Well he told me off for just being happy and messing about in the field.'

'What do you mean by "messing around," Sammy?' Lou asked.

'I was only pulling the other horses tails and chasing them,' replied Samson.

Lou could understand straight away that Bobby would have been trying to protect Samson with words of advice rather than tell him off, and he also suspected that Samson had exaggerated about Bobby, as youngsters tended to.

'Look here, Samson,' said Lou, giving him some respect.

'When Bobby and I were your age we used to be the same as you, and probably worse. We were often told off for being too lively and boisterous at times, especially if we annoyed the older horses.'

'What do you mean? Do you know Bobby?' said Samson.

'Yes I know Bobby very well and he just happens to be my best friend.'

'Oh I'm so sorry Lou, if I had known...'

'Stop right there,' said Lou sternly. 'If you had not known that Bobby is my best friend you would have told the others that he is grumpy and they would have believed you.'

Samson started to understand what Lou was trying to say, after all Bobby hadn't actually been that nasty, he had only given him a warning.

'Now then, Samson, by all means enjoy yourself and play with horses and ponies the same age as you, but promise me that you won't tell lies and I promise you that I won't tell Bobby what you called him when he comes over next week.'

'He's coming here?' said Samson nervously.

'Yes he is and he comes over quite often, so I suggest you show some respect when he does,' replied Lou.

'Thanks Lou, you are a real friend and I'm sorry that I made you angry.'

Samson walked off knowing that he needed to think twice about his actions and anything he said from now on.

***

The days flew by for Samson and as the day that Bobby would arrive came closer he became quite nervous.

Lou could see that Samson was nervous and wanted to reassure him.

'Don't worry, Sammy everything will be OK but be sure to show Bobby respect, that's all.'

When Shelley arrived with Bobby in the horsebox there was a buzz of excitement in the air as all the horses loved Bobby, he was such a handsome horse and the mares fairly swooned when he passed them.

Bobby was put in the same field as Lou, Samson and two other horses that were grazing at the top of the field.

Samson stuck close to Lou as Bobby approached and whispered up to Lou, 'What should I say to Bobby?' Lou laughed to himself, he could see Samson was shaking slightly and had a warble in his voice.

'Just stay quiet and speak when you are spoken to, but most of all relax because if you don't, Bobby will sense it and that will worry him'.

'Hey, Lou, how's it going my old friend?' Bobby asked as he reached Lou and Samson.

'Oh I'm fine thanks, Bobby, how about you?'

'Everything is great, Lou, getting plenty of exercise and winning plenty of competitions for jumping.'

'I believe you know little Samson here'.

'Yes we've met, how are you, Sammy?'

Bobby had heard about the incident at Lyn's yard and called him Sammy on purpose to see what reaction he would get.

'Samson was more nervous than he could ever remember and glanced up at Lou for moral support. Lou just gave a cursory nod to Samson as if to give him permission to speak.

'Hello, Bobby it's a pleasure to see you again.'

Samson kept his answer short as he could hear his own voice was not the same as usual, it felt to him like he was trying to talk with an apple in his mouth.

'I hope Lou and the others are treating you well and that you are behaving yourself here.' Bobby spoke reassuringly to Samson and looked him straight in the eye, but with a friendly look on his face.

Lou could see that Samson was terrified and stepped in, 'He's been great, Bobby and he's a pleasure to have around.'

Samson was relieved as he couldn't have spoken even if he wanted to.

'Now then, Samson, go and join the others as me and Bobby need to catch up on things there's a good lad.'

Samson bowed his head as if Bobby and Lou were royalty and he wandered off to join the others at the top of the field.

Bobby and Lou settled down to graze on the fresh grass and chatted about the things they had been doing. After a while they decided to have some fun and raced each other up and down the field just like the old days. Samson looked on with admiration, he could now truly understand the special relationship between Lou and Bobby.

X

HERCULES

As time went on the two friends saw each other as much as they could and rode out with Camilla on many occasions.

They looked forward to their time together, but by now Bobby had matured and had become well known in the world of show jumping. He was travelling all over the country and with sponsorship from various quarters he and Shelley were well known in the equestrian world. This meant that the two boys didn't have as much contact with each other as they would have liked.

On a beautiful Sunday afternoon John asked Alex, one of the horse owners if she and her horse Lexi would like to come out for a ride with him and Lou.

'That would be nice, John, where shall we go?'

'Let's just ride round the meadow at a leisurely pace and then up to the old barn, it's far too hot to gallop around,' John told her.

As they were on the edge of the meadow, they spotted a rider on a black and white horse approaching at full speed.

At first they were quite impressed with how the horse moved, it looked from a distance to be a huge Cob of some description and a powerful one at that.

It wasn't until the rider got closer that they could see the horse was foaming at the mouth and had wide bulging eyes. The rider had no saddle and didn't slow down, which made Lou somewhat agitated. As the rider sped by he didn't even give a cursory glance towards John and Alex, which was unusual as horse riders usually say hello at the very least.

Such was the speed of the horse and rider it was difficult for John and Alex to make out who was riding the horse, it certainly wasn't a local person or they would have met him at some point.

'Do you know him?' John asked Alex.

'No, perhaps he's new around here' Alex said as she looked at John.

John made sure to look at the markings on the horse as best he could. 'As they rode on John and Alex were somewhat concerned for the horses welfare, it was being worked far harder than it should have been on this very warm afternoon.

Lou had become quite unsettled and had seen something that John and Alex hadn't. Lou had seen the face of the person on the horse and knew that it was the boy who had mistreated Rosie and who had caused him so much harm all those years ago. As much as he wanted to chase the boy who had now grown into a big man, he knew it would be dangerous.

As they rode back to the yard, Lou's eyes and ears were very alert. He was trying to pick up a trace or some kind of clue as to where this tormentor had gone.

Two weeks later Shelley and Bobby came to visit for a couple of days and Lou told Bobby all about the encounter.

'Right Lou, that's it, he can't be far from here so let's make sure we find out who the horse is for starters.'

'Put the word around all your friends and ask them who has a black and white horse that's about seventeen hands with great big furry feet.

During Bobby's visit they were both in the field and Lou decided that they should have some fun. He walked up behind Bobby while Bobby was grazing and minding his own business, and then Lou grabbed Bobby's tail with his teeth and gave it a hard tug.

Bobby raised his head immediately and looked round somewhat startled although not hurt.

'Got you there, Bobby didn't I?' Lou said as he ran off across the field.

'Bet you can't catch me,' he said as he galloped off.

Bobby immediately ran after Lou, neighing and bucking as he went.

'I'll catch you, Lou, and when I do your tail will be mine.'

The two boys played this game for a couple of hours without even knowing that all of the other horses were watching on with delight.

Bobby's visit was soon over and he was taken back to his own yard.

'Now don't forget what I said Lou, make sure you get the word out about that horse, and I will see you soon to decide what we can do,' Bobby told him before he left.

***

As the word went out around the local horse community, it wasn't long before Lou had a lead.

'Lou,' said Dash, one of the new ponies in the stables. 'That horse you need to know about lives down by the river next to the railway arch.'

'How do you know that?' said Lou, ears pricked up and looking at Dash with interest. 'Well, before I moved here I lived on the other side of the river and I saw him arrive just a day or so before I left.'

'Do you know who owns him Dash?'

'All I know is that he is tied up all day with a huge chain around his neck which is attached to a great big iron rod in the ground.' Dash was scared about telling Lou about the horse as he didn't like to be seen as a trouble maker but he felt sorry for the big horse.

'I've seen the owner hit him and sometimes his chain is too short for him to get to the water to drink.' Dash could see that Lou was listening to his every word. 'Please don't tell anyone that I told you, Lou, I don't want any trouble.'

'Don't worry Dash no one will ever know, but you must always look after other horses if you think they are in trouble.'

Lou left things at that and now that he knew where to find the horse and the rider, it was his turn to hatch a plot to capture the villain at last.

Although Billy and his mum had been sentenced to six months in prison they only served three months due to good behaviour, which angered Suzie when she found out.

Billy had grown into a big man now and didn't look at all like he did when he was sentenced, which is why John had not recognised him as he rode past on the big black and white horse.

Lou relayed the details to Bobby when he and Shelley visited a couple of weeks later. Bobby was a thinker and listened intently but Lou had learnt a great deal from Bobby over the years and had already worked out a plan to get John and Shelley to ride to the river.

Alex decided to join in the ride with John and Shelley and the three horses and riders set off down the lane. 'When they reached the fork in the path, one way led to the woods and the other to the river, Alex turned towards the wood.

Lexi had been told about the plan to get to the big black and white horse and was told by Lou to refuse to go towards the woods. Lexi was happy to help Lou in any way she could if it meant saving a horse from being treated cruelly.

Lexi planted her feet firmly on the ground and refused to move, despite Alex trying to urge her on.

'That's strange' Alex said as she tried in vain to get Lexi to move, 'I've never had a problem with her going to the woods before.' Lexi stood her ground and turned away from the path towards the other direction.

'Whoa, Lexi, what's got into you?' Alex said in a loud but controlled voice. She was an expert rider and had never seen Lexi act like this.

'Let me go first, Alex, perhaps something that we didn't see spooked her.'

Shelley kicked Bobby on and after just a few steps Bobby also refused to move.

'What's got into them?' Shelley remarked. 'Come on, Bobby, walk on,' Shelley said sharply. Bobby was having none of it and turned away just as Lexi had, Shelley tried to turn him back but such was Bobby's strength and determination Shelley had to give in.

'You go first Dad,' Shelley said, 'perhaps you will have better luck than us.

John moved Lou into position and tried the same thing but Lou stood firm. 'Come on, Lou, walk on there's a good lad'. Lou knew there was only one thing for it and rose up on his hind legs just enough to give John a scare but not enough to put him in danger.

'What's happening here', John yelled as Lou's front end came down. Lou turned towards Lexi and Bobby who were standing quite still.

'I think we ought to take the other route today, there's clearly something wrong that only the horses can sense.'

The three horses and riders set off towards the river, but there was still another choice of direction further on and Lou was just hoping that they wouldn't have to repeat the same thing.

When they reached the junction where one direction led to the meadows and the other led to the river the horses were relieved to hear Alex suggest that they go down to the river and let the horses have a drink. It was a warm day and there were some sections of the river that were good to ride in.

Riding in water was somehow exciting to the riders and it helped to cool the horses down when the water splashed up under their bellies and on their legs.

When they arrived at the river there was only one direction that they could go. A road had been built over the river and the bridge was too low for them to get under.

They set off towards the railway bridge that they could see way off in the distance. As they walked through the water, Alex and Shelley were discussing the problem they had earlier on and couldn't come up with any good reason for all three horses to refuse like that.

Parts of the river were quite deep and the water came up to the bottom of the saddles, it was quite exciting and the riders were glad that they had been led to the river by the horses, which made them laugh when they discussed it.

'Perhaps the horses wanted a dip,' said Alex with a chuckle.

After about ten minutes they were close to the railway bridge, which had a huge brick column blocking the view to the field beyond. As they passed the column, they were surprised to see the big black and white horse that Alex and John had seen when they were riding out a couple of weeks before.

'Oh my god, look at the sores around that horses neck,' Shelley said.

They rode out of the river and dismounted.

'Let's tie the horses up to that tree and check this horse out,' Shelley said.

After tying the horses up the three of them approached the horse carefully as he was very big and his ears were pricked up as if in fright.

'Steady boy,' Shelley said in a calm voice as she approached the horse. She could see that the horse had been tied up for some time as the chain had worn away the hair around his neck. The horse was calm and could sense that Shelley was not a threat to him, he allowed her to examine him all over.

'This horse is underweight for his height and his teeth need filing,' Shelley said to her dad and Alex.

She checked his feet and could tell immediately that his hooves had not been picked for a long time.

There was no sign of any water buckets or hay and it was obvious by the state of the river bank that the horse was constantly being moved onto the next post once he had eaten all the grass. She led the horse towards the river and was shocked that the chain was too short by only two feet, the poor horse could only smell the water.

The chain was padlocked around the horse's neck and it was secured to a metal hoop at the top of a large metal stake which had been driven into the ground.

'Let's get back to the yard and get Suzie on the phone, this horse cannot be allowed to live like this any longer.'

The three of them mounted their horses and rode back to the stables as fast as they could.

'Well, Bobby, that was a great result,' Lou said as soon as they had been un-tacked and put in the field.

Shelley telephoned Suzie when she had put the horses out and explained things to her.

'Don't worry, Shelley, we will be there within the hour and I will have an RSPCA officer with me. Just get down there and make sure that the horse gets some hay and water, but be sure that you take care and if anyone can see you just wait for us before you do anything.'

Shelley, John and Alex drove down to the area and parked up as close as they could to where the horse was tethered.

They looked around and as the area was not overlooked by any property they felt happy to proceed.

They took with them a five gallon drum of water and a large bucket, together with a large bag of hay. The grass where the horse was tied up was all eaten and there was a track where the horse had been walking in circles trying to get what little shoots of grass still remained. The lack of horse droppings was a clear sign that the horse wasn't eating well.

As soon as they tipped the hay out on the ground the big horse was on it like a shot.

'Tip that water into the bucket Dad,' Shelley said, and the horse sucked up the water like it hadn't had a drink for days.

Although they were worried about the owner of the horse turning up, they were ready for it and had planned to take photographs of the people and get the number plates of any vehicles. But, as it turned out, Suzie and the RSPCA officer arrived before any owners and the officer swiftly cut the chain off of the horse's neck. Suzie had arranged for an RSPCA officer to be in attendance to act as a witness and explain to the owners (if they turned up) that they were within the law to take the horse to a place of safety.

They led the horse to the trailer and it was soon clear that they were going to have problems loading him. The usual techniques weren't working and although they had a strap behind its rump and were pulling and pushing with all their might, the horse wasn't going to go into the trailer.

'Well he seems well behaved,' said Suzie. 'What about if we walk him up to where John stables Lou and see if we can load him there or if not we can ask the stable owner if he can stay there until we work out how to get him to the sanctuary.

It was about a forty five minute walk to the stables via the country roads or a two hour walk via the bridle paths.

'I'll walk him up there with Dad,' Shelley told Suzie. 'We'll go by road as it will be much quicker.

'I will join you,' said the RSPCA officer, 'just in case there's a problem,'

Shelley, John, the RSPCA officer and one of Suzie's sanctuary volunteers, set off with the big horse down the narrow lanes.

They decided to call the horse Hercules, such was his size. He was no problem and walked by Shelley's side as if he knew he was going to a better place.

John and the RSPCA officer walked ahead to warn any oncoming cars to slow down and the volunteer walked a good way behind to warn any cars approaching from behind to slow down.

This worked well and as the few cars that did pass by drove very slowly Hercules didn't even acknowledge them, it was obvious that he had been exposed to traffic.

When they were about a mile away from where they had found him, they were rounding a corner which had a field gate to the right-hand side and a row of three terraced houses, which were set back off the road by about twenty feet. Each house had a small picket fence with a wooden gate in the middle. There were hedges to the right and left of the houses, which were about eight feet high so that any inhabitants would not have seen Hercules until he was right outside their property.

John and the RSPCA officer were about thirty feet ahead and had passed the houses when they heard someone shouting.

'Hey, where are you going with my horse?' the man's voice was deep and loud and he sounded very aggressive.

Hercules and Shelley were by this time directly outside the row of houses and were startled by the man's voice.

The man ran out to confront Shelley and hadn't seen John and the RSPCA officer who by now were walking back towards the unfolding scene.

With his well-practiced procedures, the RSPCA officer had his camera out and was capturing the scene before he had even spoken to the man.

'What seems to be the problem here, sir,' the officer politely asked the man. Without thinking of the consequences the man shouted, 'that's my horse she has there, that's the problem, and who are you to be asking me anyway?'

The man was tall and stocky with a beard and his aggressive stance made the situation seem potentially explosive, but the officer had been trained to defuse moments like this.

'Well, sir, I am an RSPCA officer and this horse has been found without water or food and the chain around his neck has caused sores that need urgent treatment.'

The man immediately changed his tone of voice and seemed to be struggling for words.

'Well it's not my horse actually, he belongs to a friend of mine and I'm just looking after him.'

It was at this point that John recognised the man - it was Billy the one who had brought so much misery to Lou and Rosie. John had seen the boy in court and although he had grown up he was recognisable by his dark curly hair and weathered features.

John decided to keep this information to himself for the moment as it was clear that Billy hadn't recognised him or Shelley despite the fact that he had seen them before at the court hearings years earlier.

John looked at Shelley and winked in the hope that she wouldn't blurt out that she recognised Billy. Shelley seemed a bit confused but John managed to whisper to her who the man was while the RSPCA officer was dealing with Billy.

'As the owner of the horse, I am going to need your details, sir, in order to either get the horse back to you if you can satisfy us that you will be making changes to his welfare, although that decision is not mine to make.'

Billy had been banned from owning animals for life and knew he had to deny owning the horse.

'As I said, officer, the horse belongs to a friend who is away at the moment.'

'But I clearly heard you say where are you going with my horse, and then you told me that's your horse the young lady has there.'

'I need you to provide me with your full name and address please, sir, and I will process the paperwork and be in touch.'

The man gave the officer a false name and address and went back into the house.

'That's not his real name, officer,' John said as soon as the man had gone.

'I know that, John, we get this all the time, but thankfully we know where he lives so I will be back here later with the police to arrest him.'

As they walked the horse back to the stables, John explained to the officer about Billy's history of mistreating horses and how he had been banned from keeping any animals for life.

'Don't worry, John, this man will be arrested as soon as I can arrange it and we will get a court case going against him.'

When they got to the stable it was agreed that they would try to load Hercules onto Julian's lorry, which was much more practical for moving such a large horse.

It didn't take too much effort to load him this time with a little help from feed buckets and having a bigger lorry. Hercules was taken to the sanctuary and after initial checks it was clear that his recovery period would be much shorter than that of most of the horses that were rescued. Cobs are a very sturdy breed and this Cob was sturdier than most, despite his mistreatment.

Bobby and Lou saw Hercules arrive at the stables and were so happy that they had managed to help rescue him. Lexi was in the next field and too far away for Lou to shout to her so he started neighing and running up and down the field trying to catch her attention, which worked, but not before Shelley and John heard the commotion.

'What's got into Lou?' Shelley asked anxiously.

John and Shelley ran over to the field in case Lou was in trouble.

'Perhaps he's been stung or something,' said John who was as worried as Shelley.

By the time they got to the field Lexi had made her way over to the fence and Lou was telling her about Hercules.

'Oh that's great news Lou; it's so good to be able to help you and Bobby with your plans, do you think that he will be OK now?'

'I'm sure he will, Lexi, he will go to the sanctuary where I came from and then go to a new home.'

John and Shelley saw the two horses and assumed that they were just grooming each other and wandered off back to the stables.

*****

The following day, Shelley and her dad decided to have one last ride out together before Shelley took Bobby back to her yard.

'Do you know, Dad, I'm starting to think that Bobby and Lou are behind us rescuing Hercules and were responsible for us trying to save Rosie.'

'What makes you say that Shelley?' said John slightly puzzled.

'Do you remember Tiffany telling us how Lou and Camilla acted when they passed the house where Rosie was found, and also how Lexi, Lou and Bobby acted yesterday?' It was as if they wanted us to find Rosie and Hercules.'

The two of them rode on thinking about the possibility of the horses instigating what had happened; they didn't dismiss it.

XI

BILLY'S DAY IN COURT

The RSPCA officer kept to his word. 'To his surprise when he arrived at the house the following morning, with the police, Billy was there.

'Good morning, Mr Smith, you know why I am here and I have two police officers with me to make a formal arrest.'

'Come in, officers, I have the owner of the horse here and he can confirm that I don't own him.'

After a brief discussion, where Billy confessed to giving a false name because he was frightened, the police formally arrested him and his friend for cruelty to animals.

This was going to be a very straightforward court case as the RSPCA officer had clearly heard Billy say that it was his horse that Shelley was leading past his house.

Billy was taken into custody, while the prosecution prepared their case, because of his past convictions and the fact that he had failed to turn up to court on a previous occasion a few years before.

Billy's friend was given a strict warning from the police and RSPCA when he confessed to not being the true owner of the horse, he was told that he could get a prison sentence for mistreating a horse and this scared him off from supporting Billy's lies

The court case was prepared within a few weeks and despite Billy's solicitor putting up a case for Billy, it was of no use. With the courtroom and public gallery full the sentence was passed.

'Mr Billy Smith,' said the judge, 'You have once again shown your total disrespect for the law and have demonstrated that you have no compassion for horses.'

'By the powers invested in me, I sentence you to eight years in prison, which is the maximum term I can give you by law.'

Billy had not only been sentenced for cruelty to animals but also for his refusal to attend court, giving a false name and address and trying to pervert the course of justice.

All of this gave the judge the ability to impose a large sentence on Billy, which he deserved.

Billy's solicitor had told him that he would probably be sentenced to a maximum period of four years in prison, so it came as a complete surprise for it to be double that.

There were gasps from Billy's family and friends in the public gallery, but these were drowned out by the cheers from people who had seen many horses suffer and even die as a result of people like Billy.

Billy showed no remorse or emotion as he was led away by the court officials.

It wasn't long before the news got back to Lou and although he was glad to hear that Billy got what he deserved, he could never work out how humans could be so cruel to horses and it reminded him of what he and Rosie went through. Lou was so glad that the sanctuary was there for mistreated horses.

When Bobby found out about Billy's sentence he knew that he should try to get a message to Hercules.

Hercules had told them how he was beaten by Billy with a stick in order to gallop faster and how Billy had left him for days on end without food or water.

He told them that it was only the fact that he was moved along the river bank with the stake driven into the ground in different places from time-to-time that he got the opportunity to eat fresh grass.

A little New Forest pony called Annie that had been taken from the sanctuary to Lyn's yard to be trained by Shelley, was due to return to the sanctuary on the following day.

Annie was put out in the field for the night along with Bobby and Dinky one of the livery horses.

Bobby and Annie had seen each other around the yard but hadn't really got acquainted.

'Hi, Annie, I'm Bobby, I hear you are going back to the sanctuary tomorrow.'

'Oh, hi Bobby, yes I am but only for a few weeks as Suzie has found me a new home to go to.'

Bobby told Annie about his time there and how he and his friends had helped to save Hercules, who was still at the sanctuary.

After explaining things to her in as much detail as he knew, Annie promised to carry out Bobby's wishes to the letter.

Annie was collected from Lyn's yard on the following morning and taken to the sanctuary. She was immediately put into a huge field which had as many as forty horses in it.

It was clear to Annie that the horse she needed to speak to was indeed there, he was a giant and she felt quite small and intimidated as she walked up to him.

'Hi, you must be Hercules,' Hercules lifted his head and looked down at little Annie.

'I am he,' said Hercules in a deep and slow voice, 'and who might you be?'

Annie explained who she was and she relayed word for word what Bobby had told her.

'Hmmm, I see,' said Hercules, never one to rush himself if he could help it. He was far too big and heavy to rush around or even to respond quickly, he was a thinker just like Bobby, and it was only when he was being beaten by Billy did he ever have to rush.

'Well, my little friend,' he said with a smile on his face 'you have certainly cheered me up this day, thank you.'

Hercules left it at that and wandered off, he was a horse of few words, but Annie could see that he was pleased with the news.

Annie went off and spread the news about Billy to the other horses and it wasn't long before they all knew. Some of the horses that had been at the sanctuary for years remembered Billy and what he had done to Lou and Rosie and they too were pleased with the news.

XII

A VERY HAPPY REUNION

Five years passed by with Bobby and Lou being brought together for weekends of riding and on occasion they would be taken down to the South Coast where they would be treated to a day on the beach. They loved riding into the water with John and Shelley on their backs and galloping along the beach in the surf.

'It was on one of these days out to the beach that they saw a horse and rider coming towards them in the distance.'

As they approached each other Shelley and her dad commented on how nice the other horse looked.

Lou and Bobby had seen the horse and rider approaching, but were enjoying the day so much that they weren't paying too much attention.

'Hi there,' said Shelley as they were within hearing range of the other rider.

'Hello,' replied the lady who rode the beautiful bay horse.

At that point her horse gave out the loudest neigh that she had ever heard.

Lou and Bobby were startled by the noise and immediately raised their heads and halted.

'Whoa, what's got into you, Hope?' said the lady.

With that Lou started neighing and raced forward to the horse that was making so much noise in front of him.

Bobby looked on in bewilderment. Lou's reaction was so strong that John struggled to hold on to him. It had been nearly fourteen years since Lou was taken from his mother at eight months old and here they were rubbing their cheeks together. Hope recognised Lou immediately. Her mother's intuition was confirmed by his markings, his dark mane and tail, the little white stripes on his nose and those long eyelashes.

Lou in turn had recognised his mum, but it had been so many years he had almost forgotten what she looked like. Horses have a much stronger sense of these things than their owners and this above anything else radiated out of them both.

'Oh my, I don't believe it, exclaimed Atalia. That's Jack isn't it?'

The last thing that Atalia expected to see was the little foal that Hope had given birth to all those years ago.

John was trying to pull Lou away from Hope but without any success.

'No this is Lou,' said John somewhat bemused.

'I can tell you now that my horse, Hope, is the mother of the horse you have there,' said Atalia 'and I can only think that someone has changed his name at some point.'

Atalia started to dismount to take a closer look at Lou.

From where she had been sitting on Hope, she couldn't quite see Lou's right-hand side and wanted to see if he had a mark on his belly.

'As I recall' Atalia said to John 'Jack had a white mark on his belly just to the right hand side, and from the way these two horses are behaving it's clear that there is something going on.'

'Dad,' said Shelley, 'just look at the likeness of them both, it could be possible'.

Sure enough, it was just as Atalia had thought all along, as soon as she saw the white mark on Lou's belly she knew.

Atalia gave Lou a cuddle and he in turn nuzzled up to her as if he had known her forever. Despite the time that had passed by and the fact that Atalia was now a lady, he did recognise her.

Once they had all dismounted they walked the horses over to the sand dunes where there were some grassy banks for them to graze on. After introductions were made they started to discuss the past.

Atalia was really sorry to hear about what had happened to Lou but she was also glad to hear that since being rescued he had made a full recovery and was enjoying life to the full.

'Oh, Mum, it's so nice to see you again,' Lou said as he was grooming Hope.

'I never thought we would meet again but I always thought about you wherever I was.'

'I thought the same too, Jack, and I must say what a handsome horse you have become.'

Lou explained to his mother that the family who had bought him didn't really know how to manage horses so he decided to leave and went to the sanctuary and they decided to change his name.

Bobby was grazing just a short way from Lou and Hope and although he didn't want to pry on what they were saying, he just hoped that Lou wasn't going to tell her about what had happened to him while he was with Billy.

Lou had learnt so much from Bobby and he knew that his mother Hope would feel so sad if she knew what he had been through, so he decided to keep the painful memories to himself.

Lou did see Bobby give him a quick glance as if to say 'be careful what you say, Lou,' but Bobby had always been the one that Lou told his innermost thoughts to and that's how it would remain.

While the horses were enjoying their grazing and getting acquainted, Shelley, John and Atalia chatted about the horses and how often they would visit the beach.

After an hour the three of them exchanged details and planned to meet the following month. They were only fifteen miles away from each other and it would be easy to get together for rides out or to travel to the coast for days out.

As they parted Lou and Hope rubbed their necks together and as they had overheard Shelley and Atalia say they would meet again next month, they didn't part with a broken heart as they had done all those years ago.

As Lou and Bobby galloped along the beach they neighed out loud and in return Hope responded.

Of all the days and years that had passed, this day was the happiest day that Lou and Bobby could ever remember.